POP CITY

POP CITY

BULLETS AIN'T GOT NO NAMES

A Work of Fiction

By

THOMAS DUANE-TAYLOR

ISBN: 978-1-63751-558-7

Dedication

This first book is dedicated IN THE LOVING MEMORY of my mother, Edna Fay Taylor. I love you Moms, may you rest in Peace.

Chapter 1

Our story begins in the notorious depths of Newark "Brick City" New Jersey, between Clinton Avenue and Clinton Place.

It was summertime, and Rock was awakened by the sun blazing through a slit in the blue custom Polo drapes. He had a massive headache from the wild night before of partying, drinking, and smoking weed.

Rock reluctantly got up, squinting in a half-hearted attempt to shield his sensitive dark brown eyes from the unwanted intrusion of the offensive sun.

He stood up wearing nothing more than a pair of black Gucci boxers and a Jamaican colored hairnet, to protect his long dark red locks. With a brief stretch of his 6 foot, 185 pound frame, he made his way over to the mahogany dresser and gave himself a once over in the mirror. His abs were slacking a little bit, and he made a mental note to make it to the gym that week and tighten up.

Rock struck up a Newport and was startled by movement in the corner of the room. *What the fuck was that?* he thought to himself as he squinted his eyes in an attempt to better focus on the suspicious slim figure laying comfortably in his bed underneath the silk Polo sheets.

The hairs on the back of his dark neck raised as he spoke in the strongest, most manliest tone his Henny stricken voice could muster, "BITCH GET THE FUCK OUT . . . IT'S CHECKOUT TIME."

The sexy feline figure slowly rustled to lean up in the bed, as the silk sheet fell to her waistline, revealing perfectly sized caramel-colored breasts and hard erect nipples.

"Good morning," Lanceen said through beautiful lips and a million dollar smile to match.

Her long, jet black hair appeared slightly tousled, giving her a sexy jungle cat look.

Just as Rock thought that things couldn't get any better, Lanceen squatted onto her knees, the sheet fell almost completely away from her naked body, revealing thick, beautiful hips attached to a rock hard stomach.

"What you say, baby?" she questioned him in a roundabout casual way, while reaching her arms up to yawn and stretch.

As his sexual excitement grew, using his best Barry White impression, "I was just asking you if you comfortable . . . baby?"

He mentally patted himself on the back at the slick response and quick thinking on his part.

Damn this girl is fine, Rock thought to himself as he focused on her high cheek bones and tiger slit eyes.

"I'd be even more comfortable if you was laying next to me, or better yet laying in me," Lanceen said with lust in her voice and a slight grin on her face.

Rock stalked over to the bed and sat down between her thick thighs. He then took her face into his hands and began tongue kissing her with the expertise of a Frenchman.

Lanceen responded by leaning back, reaching through the slit in his boxers and taking his manhood into her hands and massaging it gently.

Rock climbed on top of her, Lanceen opening her legs and guiding his massive penis into her hot awaiting pussy.

Her love nest was tight, wet and sticky. So tight in fact that only seconds upon entering her he found himself ready to explode prematurely. Saving himself the embarrassment of having been called a minute man, Rock decided to withdraw his tool.

Just when I was getting into it, Lanceen thought to herself. She clumsily grabbed at his hips. However, the sweat from their brief lovemaking had soaked through his boxers, making it impossible for her to hold on.

Rock softly kissed and sucked on her erect nipples, before trailing down her stomach, finally resting on her vagina. Once there, he spread Lanceen's thick legs apart with his muscular arms. Satisfied that her legs were spread apart enough, Rock took her into his mouth. One at a time, he traced her swollen pussy lips, maneuvering his head and big, moist tongue, capturing every droplet of her succulent nectar, driving her crazy in anticipation.

Unable to take anymore teasing, Lanceen took a handful of his locks and forced his hot mouth onto her agitated clitoris, as if force-feeding an uncooperative toddler. Minutes later Lanceen was gyrating her thick hips to the rhythm of his tongue and at the same time releasing her orgasm down his awaiting throat.

Got her, he thought to himself, as he finished his meal in record time. Now for the main course.

Lanceen trembled in erotothermic fashion as Rock roughly flipped her onto her stomach and entered her from behind. After getting over the initial shock of his manhood, Lanceen clamped down on Rock's penis and pushed her plump, firm ass up in rhythm to meet his hard, deep thrusts.

After thirty minutes of hard lovemaking, Rock once again felt himself ready to explode, when suddenly he heard a loud banging on his front door.

Rock wanted to ignore the intrusion. However, exhausted from fucking, Lanceen insisted that he answer the door, promising that they would continue their lovemaking session when he gets rid of their unwanted guest.

Rock reluctantly got up, adjusted his boxers, then slowly walked barefoot to his front door. He could feel plush carpet underneath his feet, as he walked into the living room.

When he peered out of the peephole, there was another loud bang on the door, followed by the voice of his childhood friend and crime partner, Reek.

"Rock OPEN THE FUCKEN DOOR . . . IT'S URGENT." Rock opened the door partially and stuck his head out, not wanting to expose his friend to all the sweet that drenched his body due to his most recent activities.

"DAMN NIGGA YOU SWEATEN LIKE YOU BEEN IN SOME PUSSY OR SOMEN," Reek joked as he pushed the door open, then playfully jabbed Rock in his exposed stomach. "You need to lose some weight my dude," Reek added.

Rock put on a mock expression of pain on his face, as he returned the gesture, lightly punching Reek in his ribs. "Exactly," Rock answered with a more serious look on his face.

"Whatever," Reek replied. His face also becoming more serious as he thought of the grim report that he had to tell his best friend.

They both paused in an awkward silence, as Rock impatiently awaited the news that was so important that it had gotten him out of some good pussy.

Reek inhaled a deep breath of fresh air into his short 5 foot 8 inch frame and prepared himself to tell his best friend the bad news.

Well, here goes nothing, he thought to himself as he blurted out the problem. "Rock, we got beef with them Prince street nigga's."

"Just as one beef ends, another one begins," Rock mumbled under tightly clenched teeth. "WHAT THE FUCK IS THE PROBLEM NOW?"

Before Rock could say another word, he noticed Reek's mouth gaping open and wondered what had caught his attention, especially at such a stressful moment.

Rock turned to see what was capturing Reek's attention and saw a sexy Lanceen squeeze by him and walk down the steps in a tight mini-skirt and halter top with Channel purse and heels to match.

Before jumping into her white supped-up GS-400 and pulling off, she looked over her shoulder and said in a seductive, yet whiny voice, "Rock, you took too long . . . I'll see you later."

"How am I going to see you later when I just met you last night and I don't even know your address," he thought to himself.

Pissed off, he reluctantly waved Reek in, who was still trying to catch another look at Lanceen's fat ass.

Rock closed and locked the door, as Reek flopped on the leather couch in his usual spot.

"Roll up nigga," Rock said over his shoulders as he walked into the bedroom and put his platinum Movado watch, chain, timbs and loose-fitting jeans on.

Though the year was two thousand and twelve, being an eighties baby, Rock refused to indulge in what he regarded as the fruity skinny jeans fashion, and instead elected to wear his jeans loose, but form fitting.

Rock sat next to his boy Reek and toyed with his watch and glimpsed Reek completing the task of rolling up the weed blunt.

Rock, oftentimes, played with his jewelry. I suppose growing up poor had caused him to appreciate more of the things that he did have.

They played video games on the couch, while smoking on the most powerful weed that Newark had to offer, 1.89. For the moment, they relaxed and forgot all their problems, blowing their worries away between thick powerful clouds of weed smoke.

Suddenly, Reek and Rock's favorite past-time was interrupted by what sounded like someone kicking at the base of the front door.

"WHO THE FUCK IS IT?" Rock questioned with contemptuous disrespect in his voice.

Reek, jumped up and answered the door at the same time that the disrespectful interrupter responded. "IT'S SANTA CLAUSE . . . MA FUCKER OPEN UP."

Clarence Tay Moore, a.k.a. Bullet, was the tallest member of the Prince Street Posse Bloods.

He wondered what had him standing in front of a nigga's house that he didn't even know, and why he was told to bring his brand new Tech-9.

In fact, out of the people that were standing there on the porch, Bullet had only known one of them—a short fat loudmouth, Raheem, who was at the moment claiming to be Santa Clause, nervously holding two 3.80 cal. handguns near his waistband.

Oh well, better safe than sorry, Clarence thought to himself while cocking back on the lever located on the side of his new Tech-9.

Everybody on the porch seemed ready for war and armed to the teeth with weapons. The other two men carried nine-millimeters and .45 caliber semi-automatic handguns.

The w hole scene reminded Clarence of a S.W.A.T. team raid. All doubts and questions left Bullet when the door to the two-family dwelling swung open and all hell broke loose.

Raheem bullied his way past the shorter, smaller Reek, shooting him twice in the upper chest. He entered the dark room and surveyed it with his guns.

Meanwhile, Bullet was not as prepared like he previously determined.

Everything seemed to develop so quickly, too quickly in fact for Bullet, because as he entered the house, trailing the two other men, he fumbled with his gun and almost dropped it. Bullet was barely in the front door when he heard the loudest sound that he had ever heard in his entire short life.

The sound of a double-barreled shotgun discharging in a confined place will do that.

It took a long moment for Bullet's eyes to adjust from the sunlight to the eerie darkness of Rock's living room, yet still, through the light of the television he could have sworn that he had seen a shadowy figure press a button on the couch, retrieve what appeared to be a large shotgun and blow his friend Raheem's head clean off of his shoulders.

Scared and confused the two other men shot blindly into the house as the shadowy figure darted back and forth, from one end of the room to the next, all the while seeming to get closer.

Rock used the men's confusion to his advantage. When the double-barrel slugs hit them at close range, the men were simultaneously lifted off of their feet. So high, in fact, that Bullet imagined their heads had crashed into the ceiling.

Bullet felt hot blood and warm flesh slash his face and eyes, almost blinding him instantly. He then felt something similar to a slug hammer hitting him at full force in his lower back, as he attempted to run, which caused him to throw his gun in the air and trip over his own feet.

He could hear a faint wheezing, a labored breathing type sound in the distance.

Damn, some poor bastard was having a hard time catching his breath, he thought comically to himself. What, was that him making that noise? Struggling to catch his breath, he attempted to, without success to get to his feet, reality setting in that he was the one who was shot.

He could feel warm blood pouring down his back and legs. He could hear the distinctive sounds of timberland boots on a wooden porch slowly approaching him.

Was the angel of death coming to gently lift his soul from his body? *Couldn't be,* he thought to himself. The angel of death would never have been so disrespectful as to spit on him, curse at him, and violently kick him in his neck and head with the heel of his boots.

Rock stood over the limp man's body, aggressively stomping him in his head, with his shotgun in his hand and tears rolling down his face.

Rock was venting the passing of his best friend and crime partner, causing him to temporarily go insane. He had lost all sense of time. He could no longer tell how long he had been there, standing on his porch half-dressed, stomping the lifeless corpse of his enemy.

The only thing that had awakened him from his trance like rage, was the gruesome sounds of bone breaking under the weight of his feet.

Rock wiped the sweat from his face and brow, as he surveyed the surrounding area, hoping to no avail that no one had seen or heard what just happened.

He heard the sounds of feet shuffling at the top of the staircase, no doubt the nosy couple he rented his upstairs apartment to.

He could now visualize middle-aged Luna, standing nervously in her leopard print housecoat and fuzzy pink slippers, chattering away to a 911 operator about how their drug dealing king pin of a landlord was stomping a man to death on their front porch, with a loaded shotgun in his hands.

Luna didn't care about the fact that Rock was just defending himself and his property. The only thing that registered in her mind was that he was a drug dealer and all drug dealers are evil.

Rock quickly retrieved the dead man's Tech-9 from the steps, then darted by the other fallen men, stopping briefly over the motionless body of his boy Reek. He thought of checking his limp body for vital signs, then thought against it. Reek was dead and no amount of hope could ever bring him back.

He quickly ran into his bedroom, looking back and forth. He grabbed a black duffle bag from his closet and placed the Tech-9 and shotgun into it.

"I gotta get the fuck outta here," he mumbled to himself, as he put on a black Polo shirt with a black and gray velour jacket.

Before leaving, he reached into his dresser drawer, grabbing his black .40 caliber pistol, placing it in his waistband, truck keys, duffle bag, wallet, then jetting out of the house.

He briefly regarded his truck. He had low profile Pirelli tires and black custom made 23-inch rims to match. He was the only one in the hood with a 2011 Range Rover sitting on 23's in the rear of the truck and 22's in the front. Dreamworks Auto Body Shop had to re-configure the entire suspension system just to compensate for the rear to front wheel differential. He also paid a grip to turbocharge the engine.

He jumped into his truck and was greeted b the black butter soft leather seats that he had the name of his record label "Body Count" etched into. He pressed the start button and tossed the duffle bag into the rear seat.

The truck's powerful V-12 turbo-charged engine roared to life without hesitation.

In the past year he had thought of trading in his old Range for the newer model, however had decided against it, reasoning that he had already invested entirely too much money into the one he had.

As he put the pedal to the floor, he heard the sound of the rear tires screech. He pulled out of the parking space and thanked GOD that he decided to keep his truck.

Not paying attention, Rock roared through a yellow lighted intersection, only realizing his mistake upon hearing the sounds of the police siren behind him.

Damn, he thought to himself. He's only made it four blocks away from his, which was currently a whirlwind crime scene. He contemplated on whether or not to pull over, or to give the lone police officer a run for his money. However, he decided against it, reasoning that the officer's walkie-talkie was faster than his supped-up V-12.

Rock reluctantly pulled over, making sure to pick a spot near the sidewalk that was void of other cars, just in case he had to go with his first idea.

He adjusted his rearview mirror in order to catch a better look at the cop as he stealthily slid his .40 cal from his waistband and tucked it, cocked, between the center console and driver's seat.

As the black officer approached his driver's side door, Rock cursed him underneath his breath, then attempted to put on his best. "Officer, I never saw that red light back there," face on. A face that apparently only worked for women.

The cop looked at him with contempt, hatred and jealousy in his eyes and said, "Boy you know you ran a red light back there in that intersection. What's the emergency?"

Rock thought quickly. "Well officer, what happen was, my wifey is having a bay and . . ."

The officer rudely cut him off and said, "Boy that's no reason to endanger the public." He paused, then continued. "License, registration and insurance."

Though Rock was growing tired of that "boy" shit, he took his hand off of his pistol and began to ramble through his truck, trying to buy enough time to think himself out of his situation.

I'll pay him off, Rock thought to himself. I wonder if this joker takes checks.

Just as he opened up his wallet, intent on paying the cop off, the officer received a frantic call over the radio. "CAR 43-CAR43, WE HAVE A 1.8.7 ON CLINTON AVENUE AND CLINTON PLACE . . ." A pause, then the 911 operator continued, "WHERE YOU AT?"

"Today's your lucky day boy. Now get the fuck out of here and go have that baby," the officer ordered Rock as he ran back to his squad car, turned his siren on and pulled off.

Rock waited a moment, then pulled off himself, thanking GOD that he had gotten out of that one.

He knew that the Courts wouldn't accept his self-defense claim, so there was no reason to turn himself in. The jury would have found him guilty base don his record alone. Besides, Rock only had one strike left, which meant that he would have gotten sentenced to life or worse, which was death. Rock shuddered at the possibility of the electric chair.

He was no Johnny Cochran, but he had known enough about the law to know that his chances were slim to none that he would walk out of that courtroom without a scratch.

The light on his expensive dashboard indicated that he was low on gas, so he decided to go to the gas station on Central Avenue. He pulled up on pump number three, jumped out of his truck, placed the nozzle in, pressed the lever, then walked into the store, leaving the truck running.

Rock went to the counter with three C and C soda cans in his hands and a bag of cheese doodle chips.

"Yo, let me get $25.00 on pump 3, two duchies and a pack of Newport's . . . Oh yeah, and that blue lighter," Rock added as an afterthought.

He paid with a fresh fifty dollar bill and told the store clerk to keep the change, in hopes that the extra money would be enough incentive for him to disregard the large bulge of his forty caliber hidden in his waistband along with the Tech-9.

As Rock was exiting from the store he would have sworn that he saw what looked like a man jumping into the driver's side of his truck. However, Rock quickly dismissed that idea, arrogance in his tough street cred not allowing him to believe that somebody was brave or stupid enough to rob him.

As he got closer, reality set in and it was someone, a skinny guy that jumped into his truck. Rock yelled at the top of his lungs, "YO GET THE FUCK OUT OF MY FUCKEN TRUCK."

His words only caused the skinny guy to panic even more. The guy's heart literally skipped a beat when he saw Rock pull out the biggest handgun that he had ever seen in his entire life.

The guy's intentions was to only search the truck for some loose change or something else of value so he could get high that day, not get himself killed.

However, with a tall, black man running towards him with a hand cannon, his plans had changed dramatically.

As with all of GOD's gentle creatures, survival was the first law of nature, so with that in mind, the guy did what most men would have done in that situation. He put the truck into gear and pulled off, breaking the gas pump and leaving a waterfall of gasoline shooting into the air in his wake.

The hose looked similar to a snake with its head cut off, the way it violently swayed back and forth gushing gasoline all over the gas station.

Rock took aim and discharged three shots at the truck's rearview window, shattering it to pieces, as it quickly exited the gas station and recklessly roared up Central Avenue out of view.

Rock could see in his peripheral that the store clerk was already on the phone, no doubt reporting the entire incident to the police.

Chapter 2

Federal Bureau of Investigation agent, Ms. Lanceen Howard Diggins, upon leaving Rock's house, had drove directly to the F.B.I. Headquarters, located in downtown Newark, for her weekly report.

She felt overconfident that she had been doing a good job and prayed that she would continue to do a good job in spite of falling for the very same suspect she had been assigned to investigate.

She never thought that after only one lovemaking session with Duane Maleek Roberts, a.k.a. Rock, she would be turned completely out.

She also never thought that such intense pleasure could come from a man. The way Rock had eaten her pussy, one would think he was part amphibian.

He really knew his way around a woman's body, Lanceen thought to herself, as her thought was rudely interrupted by her superior.

"LANCEEN GET YOUR HEAD IN THE GAME, I ASKED YOU A QUESTION," her fat, bald-headed Superior said in a commanding voice.

"Sa . . . sorry sir. I didn't hear you," Lanceen replied.

"WHERE IS OUR SUSPECT LOCATED AT THIS VERY MOMENT?" he asked again, while repeatedly slamming his pale white hand on his desktop for more dramatic effect.

"THAT DRUG DEALING BLACK BASTARD JUST MURDERED THREE PEOPLE AT HIS HOUSE DIS MORNING," he continued.

Lanceen's heart sank into the lower depths of her stomach upon hearing this news. She couldn't believe her ears. Rock couldn't have just murdered three people; she was just with him.

"Are you sure sir?" she bravely questioned.

"OF COURSE I'M SURE . . . THE NEWS JUST CAME OVER THE POLICE SCANNER TWENTY MINUTES AGO."

Lanceen, being highly aware that her Superior was well trained in spotting when one of his Agents was emotionally compromised, was careful in framing her next response. "SIR, I CANNOT TELL YOU WHERE THAT BASTARD IS AT THE MOMENT, BUT I ASSURE YOU THAT HE WILL NOT GET AWAY."

"WELL, THEN GET THE HELL OUT OF MY OFFICE AND GO CATCH HIM," Lanceen's Superior said with a hint of encouragement in his voice.

Good, he bought it, Lanceen thought to herself, as she jumped into her car and pulled off recklessly into oncoming traffic, almost hitting an elderly white lady driving a gray Fleetwood Cadillac. The older woman abruptly stopped to avoid a collision, blew her horn in protest, then flipped her the bird before rejoining traffic.

Lanceen thought of running the old bitch in, for if nothing else, wearing a white, yellow and gray flower printed dress with a pink church-style hat, but quickly decided against it, knowing that she had bigger fish to fry.

Wait a minute, she thought to herself, Mike said that Rock hasn't been captured yet; maybe I could get to him before anyone else.

After capture, she'd wonder in her mind how the conversation would go between Rock and her, when she told him that she worked for the Feds, and that she wanted to be with him.

She ran through different scenarios in her mind. The first one being, she would have to capture him in a hotel or something. She would have him sit down after making sweet love to him, looking him in those beautiful chinky brown eyes of his and just blurting it out, "Baby ... I'm a federal agent, but I love you and I want to be with you forever.

He would have kissed her and told her how much he loved and understood her, and most of all, how proud he was of her for coming clean with him and how he respected her honesty.

Then they would have lived happily ever after. Okay, maybe not that exact same way, but you get the gist. Lanceen just knew in her heart of hearts that Rock would understand, and if he didn't, she would have to just give him no other choice.

Lanceen also imagined an alternative scenario, where Rock had refused to cooperate with her plans. The dialogue would most likely go opposite her initial thoughts. She would have sat him down and broke the news to him that she was a federal agent. Rock would have gotten extremely upset, in which case she would have attempted to reason with him. If all else failed, she would have no other choice, but to blackmail him by threatening to turn him in if he didn't want to be with her.

For Lanceen it was all or nothing. Either he would choose her or life in the pen.

In any case, Lanceen knew that she held all the cards, and she was a master at playing the game.

While cruising down West Market Street, Lanceen considered going to Rock's house, however quickly, but dismissed that because Rock was too clever to be there.

She'd also considered pounding the streets and getting in touch with her secret informants, however dismissed that ideas as well, knowing that none of them were actually stupid or brave enough to rat him out.

If she knew nothing else about her suspect, she knew that he had a murderous appetite for killing snitches. Besides, she thought, Rock was too organized and disciplined to allow such a person to infiltrate his inner circle.

God how she loved him. Rock was a strong black man who had made it in spite of his circumstances.

When Lanceen had first taken on the case a couple of months ago, she'd been on surveillance for months before she figured out his weakness—pussy!

Before that first encounter with him, Lanceen had watched him for months. Actually she had fallen for him way before Rock had ever touched her. She'd helplessly watched as he dropped off weed and cocaine in large amounts to his inner city runners.

On the flip side, she'd also witnessed him beat a man to death with his bare hands, just for disrespecting an elderly black woman that he didn't even know.

She'd also seen Rock kill men by way of old-fashioned drive-by's, as he wore black gloves and a ski mask, when he got out of his car and stood over his victim and shot him with his Uzi machine gun he held in his hands. Don't ask why, but Lanceen could tell it was him. Maybe it was his posture and slim, sexy frame that gave him away, but somehow she knew it was him.

However, it wasn't the money, the glamourous lifestyle or the excitement of the murders that he'd committed that caused her to fall in love with him. It was the way in which he conducted himself as a man and the way he had chosen to spend his money that did it.

Lanceen being a good little federal agent had delved deeply into his financial records and had discovered that not only did he own a recording studio, a couple of properties, and a truck, he also owned a daycare center.

Rock had given back to the very same community that he helped to destroy, by giving ghetto kids an afternoon place to socialize and eat for free.

He would also show up from time to time and actually give money out of his own pocket to single mothers who came to drop their kids off in order to go out and look for a job. In fact, some cases he even transported them himself to various job sites.

Indeed, Lanceen had known that underneath all of that rough exterior, Rock was actually a good man who cared about his community, in a sick drug dealer type of way, of course.

Lanceen looked at her watch. It was 8:00 p.m. and the sun was just starting to sink below the horizon. She was exhausted and tired of riding around aimlessly. She'd talked to all of her sources on the street and still no sign of Rock. So she decided to go home, curl up in front of the television and eat popcorn.

The search for her suspect slash new man was over, at least for the night.

She would pick tomorrow and maybe find some fresh leads. As Lanceen stepped into her small second floor one bedroom apartment, she fumbled with her house keys, in an attempt to catch the phone that was ringing on the other side.

Chapter 3

Rock was standing in the middle of the street, gun still in his hand, sweating profusely as he tried to think of a way to exit the unforeseen mayhem that had occurred this day.

He kicked himself in the ass, as he took the sidewalk and ran up the street fleeing the crime as fast as he could.

He couldn't believe that he had done something so stupid as to leave his keys in the truck. *Well, at least I was smart enough to grab my Tech-9 and handgun before I got out*, Rock thought to himself five blocks away from the gas station.

He felt that the big gun was fairly secured, tucked in the small of his back, as he pushed both hands, one with pistol, one without into his pockets to better conceal the handgun.

"OH SHIT THE 24." Rock said to himself, almost out of breath, as he struggled to catch the bus that threatened to pass him by.

In fact, he would have missed the bus had it not been for the help of a middle-aged black man who had seen him running and screaming for the bus and stuck out his own hand to stop it for him.

Rock thanked the man for holding the bus for him, then jumped aboard, clumsily reaching into his pockets and paying the driver with his last twenty.

He never liked to keep much money on him. Rock had also learned early on in his life that 'Brick City' nigga's loved to do stick-ups and he vowed that if they ever caught him slipping, they wouldn't get much.

In all honesty, he wouldn't have even kept that much money on him, had it not been for the fact that some stick-up kids would kill a victim off of principle that he, the victim wasted their time.

Rock knew that his city was a ruthless one. However, in his heart of hearts he still had love for it.

He had a brief flashback about the time he had found a dead body stuck in his project building incinerator. He had guessed that the body had been there for quite some time, stuck between the tenth and eleventh floors in his notoriously known projects.

His thoughts were interrupted by a big butt brown-skinned girl, who had squeezed in between him and the seat, resting her massive ass onto his crotch.

The bus was packed, so most passengers were forced to stand up. Rock and the young lady were unable to control the movements of their bodies, as the but hit bump after bump, causing them to rock back and forth, grinding one ach other in the process.

They were truly at the mercy of the driver. The young woman licked her luscious lips, then looked at him seductively, as she felt his manhood rise to the occasion and poke her in the back of her soft ass. He felt embarrassed at the lack of self-control on his end and secretly cursed his dick. However, after a few minutes he found himself starting to relax, and decided to just enjoy the ride.

All the while, unbeknownst to him there was a fat light-skinned man shooting him the dirtiest looks known to mankind. He was sitting in a seat near the back of the bus, next to the exit. *This must be this dude's girlfriend,* Rock thought to himself, as he continued to involuntarily grind on the woman with reckless abandon.

His thoughts were confirmed when the man started to send curse words in his direction. "I KNOW THAT'S NOT THAT NIGGA, ROCK RIDING THE BUS?" the man said in a raspy-type voice.

Rock attempted to encounter the foul mouth man, as he clinched his hands to his side in a tight fist.

The man persisted. "WHAT HAPPENED TO ALL THAT COKE MONEY MY NIGGA... WHAT YOU SNIFFING THAT SHIW NOW," he said while tapping a middle-aged woman seated next to him.

Moments later the sounds of Jay-Z were heard blaring from a loud radio, held by a group of rowdy teenagers in the back of the bus.

The fat man chimed in on the song and looked at Rock with a wide smirk on his jealous face. "DAMN PLAYBOY, WHERE THE FUCK IS THE HUMMER AT... THAT AIN'T NO DIAMONDS ON YOUR WATCH, WHAT THE FUCK YOU DONE TO DAT."

That was the final straw for Rock. Twenty minutes of non-stop taunting was all he could take.

Before the fat man had known it, Rock was on his ass, sliding past a group of passengers. He crept up on the unsuspecting man and rained down a barrage of lefts and rights onto the man's face and head. Hot blood splattered onto the middle-aged woman's face and shirt as she raced to get out of her seat to safety.

The sounds of music stopped abruptly as passengers from all over the bus stood up and scrambled to see who was getting their ass handed to them.

Rock was sweating profusely as he took out all of the anger and frustration that the last twenty-four hours had caused him, on the man's face. With each crushing blow he delivered, Rock thought of a different thing that had caused him stress for that particular day.

POW, I'm on the fucken run for some bullshit. POW, that crack head nigga stole my fucken hundred thousand dollar truck.

The man was not aware of it at the time, but his face had become the catalyst by which Rock had used to defend against any future bouts of depression. Knocking the man out was just what he needed. It was more therapeutic than Neosporin.

When the bus finally came to a stop, Rock casually walked through the rear exit as if nothing had happened, leaving a bloody, unconscious man in his wake.

Standing on the street corner, he struck up a fresh Newport and attempted to calm his nerves, as he surveyed the surrounding area. Much to his dismay, he was now in East Orange. He had hoped to have ridden the bus all of the way to the terminal. However, fat boy had spoiled those plans.

As he put his lighter and cigarettes back into his pant's pocket, he could feel something in the seam. He moved his hand back and forth in an attempt to discover what it was. Finally, he pulled it out, only to discover a folded piece of paper. He quickly unfolded it and was happy to see that it was Lanceen's phone number. She must have slipped it into his pant's pocket while he was outside talking to Reek.

Reek, the mere thought of his best friend almost caused him to shed a tear. However, before a tear could grace the face of this half-Jamaican born king, he crossed the street to the pay phone and placed a collect call to Lanceen's house.

She picked up on the fourth ring. "Hello?"

"Yes, I have a collect call from a . . ." The operator paused for a moment, then asked, "What is your name again sir?"

"Rock."

"Will you accept?"

Before she could get the words completely out of her mouth, Lanceen accepted the call.

Her heartbeat was racing as she took in a deep breath of air and attempted to calm herself down.

"What's up baby?" Lanceen asked him in a seductive, yet nonchalant voice. She didn't want to sound too eager.

"How you doing sweetheart, you miss me?" Rock asked, while duking his head into the phone booth and scanning the streets for the police cruisers.

"Maybe just a little," Lanceen lied.

"Just a little bit," he protested.

"Okay, alot," she said, nearly inaudible, more admitting to herself than him that she shared a connection with the man on the other end of the phone.

"What was that?" Rock probed.

"ALOT OKAY. I MISSED YOU ALOT," she said, putting her head down, finally in defeat.

That's all Rock needed to hear. "So why don't we meet up so we can finish what we started," Rock said, using his dark trademark player's voice.

Lanceen's knees grew weak as she thought of his magic stick.

"Hello?" Rock asked when he didn't hear a response. A pause, then, "Are you still there?"

"Yes baby, I'm here."

"Okay, so what's up with the what's up?" He paused for a second, choosing his next words carefully. "Give me your math and I'll be over there faster than Usain Bolt at a track meet.

She laughed, then asked, "Where you at?"

"I'm on Central Ave and Main Street," Rock replied, still on the lookout for police cars.

"You're only a couple of blocks from my house. I live on Central and Harass Street, second floor, third house on your left."

"I'm on my way," he said as he banged the phone in her ear, then hailed down a passing cab.

"1251 Harass Street fam."

The cabby pulled away from the curb, as Rock wondered how he was going to pay for his ride. *I'll get Lanceen to handle it for me*, he thought, as he scooted further down into his seat, hoping that no one could see him.

I hope she doesn't start bitching and asking too many questions, like why she had to pay for his cab and where is his truck, he thought to himself.

Of course Lanceen was nothing like that, but really Rock had no clue of who he was dealing with. He was literally walking into a situation blindly. He just needed a quiet place to lay low for a minute, gather himself and figure out his next move.

Just days ago Rock had seriously considered retiring from the game, but he never thought in a million years that retirement would come sooner rather than later.

His thoughts were interrupted by the sound of the cabbie's voice, "That'll be $21.75, please."

Rock thought quickly. "Wait right here homey. I'll go up and get that."

The Mexican cab drive had been fooled before and was very reluctant to let Rock leave without first paying his fare. However, due to his expensive looking clothes and jewelry that he wore, he decided to semi-trust him, but a small warning would not hurt.

The cabbie turned around in his seat, looked Rock squarely in his eyes and said in a very serious tone, "Make sure you come right back poppy or else we going to have a very serious problem."

The cab driver watched Rock intently, as he took the steps two at a time, then disappeared into Lanceen's building. He made a mental note of Rock's physical description and the number of the building.

After jumping off the phone with her new man, Lanceen took a hot shower and thoroughly washed her long, silky hair and body with a cherry scented bath and body wash. She gave herself a once over in her full length bathroom mirror and admired her nude wet form. Her wide, sexy hips complimented her perky "C" cup breasts and athletic frame. Besides her head, her pussy was the only part of her body that contained hair. She had shaved her legs and armpits the previous day and was now mentally patting herself on the back for a job well done.

My baby's going to love this, Lanceen thought to herself as she slid her middle finger deeply inside of herself, then put it to her nose in order to check her fragrance.

Lanceen jumped when she heard the sounds of hard knuckles banging on wood.

He's here, she thought to herself, as she licked her wet fingertips clean.

She quickly threw on a pair of six-inch heels and then answered the door in the buff. When she opened the door, Rock's jaw dropped at the sight of her beautiful body.

She had looked even more stunning than he had remembered. Her hair had curled up from the witness of the shower and her body glistened with water. She looked like a female black panther after the hunt.

Rock closed the door, then locked it behind him, all the while never taking his eyes off of Lanceen.

She closed the distance between them, kissing him passionately on his lips, then unzipping his jeans, pulled his member out and started massaging it roughly. Rock's dick stiffened in her hands. Her small fingers massaged the head of his rod and it pulsated and jumped with her every touch.

He cupped her soft wide ass with both hands and stroked it, hearing Lanceen tremble and purr in response.

She turned around doggy-style and got on all fours, then arched her back in anticipation. Rock dropped his pants, weapons and boxers down to his ankles, releasing the constraints around his erection. Then he dropped himself down and entered Lanceen from behind.

Her pussy felt tight, hot and wet. He could feel every inch of her vaginal walls contract around his member as he hit her with the death strokes.

Rock bent into her back, wrapped his strong arms underneath her shoulders, then put her in a full Nelson.

"FUCK ME DADDY," Lanceen screamed out, as she came all over Rock's dick, mixing her succulent juices with his precum.

Rock continued to bang her hard. With each stroke of his pelvis, you could hear a thunderous clap as his hips made contact with her soft rear end.

"FUCK ME IN MY ASS, " Lanceen begged as she arched her back, causing her butt to raise.

Rock slowly entered her asshole, first giving her the head, then working his entire length into her hot ass. Once completely inside of her, he paused, giving himself the chance to catch his breath and control the build up of cum that was threatening to escape his shaft at any moment.

Their bodies were sweaty and they seemed to be glued to each other. He didn't want this pleasurable moment to ever end.

Rock could tell that Lanceen had never been fucked in her ass before, by the way she winced in pain when he entered her. However, pain turns into pleasure and before she knew it, she was pushing her ass back so Rock was deeper into her ass.

"FUCK ME DADDY, FASTER... THIS FEELS SOOO GOOD," she said as she bucked back, matching Rock thrust for thrust.

"Oh shit, this ass good," Rock said as he felt himself about to cum.

BANG, BANG, BANG, somebody was knocking at the door. They both ignored it initially, however, quickly dressed themselves when the knockers identified themselves as detectives.

Rock picked up his Tech-9 from the floor, hid behind the front door and signaled Lanceen to answer the door. Lanceen was so nervous that when she bent over to pick up her bathrobe, she dropped it immediately. Her hands were shaking uncontrollably.

It was something in the look of Rock's eyes that scared her to her very core. Sure, she had experienced death before, and in some cases even caused it. However, it was something in his eyes that chilled her to her very soul.

She broke out of her trance-like state and quickly put her robe on, when Rock whispered through clenched teeth, "Get the fucken door."

Rock kind of liked Lanceen, however he decided long ago that no bitch was worth his freedom.

"Who is it?" she questioned with her hand shaking on the doorknob.

Lanceen was waiting for her F.B.I. training to kick in at any moment, but it never did.

"It's the police ma'am."

"We got a call that somebody had skipped on their cab bill, and he might fit the description of a murder suspect."

Rock's hand grew even more tense on the Tech-9. He wasn't about to go back to prison. Rock raised a finger to his lips, giving Lanceen the signal to be quiet as she answered the door.

When she opened it, there were two detectives standing in the hallway, with matching blue suits. One was white and short, while the other was tall, dark-skinned and slim. They both had their weapons drawn, but when they saw Lanceen in her terrycloth robe, they holstered their guns, deciding that she didn't pose a threat.

Still, the black detective kept his hand on his holster, not quite feeling comfortable with the situation. Even though the woman seemed to be alone and violence free, his experience taught him to never trust appearances.

"Ma'am we're just doing a routine check of everyone's apartment in the area. Do you mind if we come in?" the black detective asked.

Lanceen glimpsed at Rock standing behind the door with his gun drawn, hoping he'd give her an answer to the cop's question.

Rock shook his head no in response.

The black detective forced his way past Lanceen, then reached for his weapon. He had just cleared the entrance to her door when he felt something cold and metallic press against the back of his head and the door slam behind him.

Lanceen stood by in helpless shock as the scene developed right before her very eyes. Rock had closed the door and put the Tech-9 to the back of the cop's head all in one swift motion.

"Mike are you all right in there?" the white detective asked, as he banged and kicked on the door.

Detective Mike knew that the answer that he gave could be the difference between his life and death. "I'm fine Paul," he said, choosing his life.

"Good answer, brother," Rock said through clenched teeth.

"Rock . . . I'm only here to help you," Mike pleaded, while turning his head slightly towards him.

"Mike . . . Mike Johnson is that you?" Rock questioned as he placed his gun back in his waistband and embraced his cousin.

"What the fuck you doing here . . . I almost blew your head off," Rock said while adjusting his clothes.

As Rock was getting himself together, two shots rang out suddenly through the wooden door. One bullet grazed Lanceen's shoulder, causing her to fall awkwardly on her couch, while the other one struck the living room wall.

Lanceen fell onto the couch, then rolled off onto the floor, resting in a crouched position, hands over her head, knees secured firmly beneath her.

Rock and his cousin stood there in complete shock, as the white detective kicked down the door, tripped over Mike's foot, then fell face first into the carpet.

The impact from the crash caused him to involuntarily release his .38 cal. sending it flying into the air and resting near the back door.

"GO," Rock's cousin yelled, as the other officers descended on the small apartment, shooting first and asking questions later.

Bullets buzzed by Rock's head as he ran to the back window, crashed through it, landing awkwardly on his back. Rock's landing was partially not as hard, due to the patch of grass in Lanceen's backyard. The impact was still very painful, because he landed directly on his Tech-9.

"UGGHH!" Rock yelled, as he jumped to his feet, then darted from side to side in an attempt to avoid the gunfire that was coming from Lanceen's back window.

The reckless officers had made it to the back window, started clearing away the fragments of sharp glass surrounding the frame and began raining a barrage of gunfire at the suspected killer.

Their logic was that no murder suspect would ever go peacefully, especially when he was accused of murdering multiple people and had a jacket as bad as Rock did.

Rock moved with the expertise of a Vietnam vet, first dipping his body low, using the high grass and darkness for cover, the moving at a steady pace, careful not to disturb the area around him.

He knew that the police were shooting blindly at the moment and they would find their target once he emerged from the weeds to climb over the gate. Rock waited until he was twenty yards from the gate, before he stood up and broke into a fast sprint.

The gate was approximately five feet high, but with the sounds of bullets buzzing by his ears as motivation, Rock was able to leap the gate in one bound, barely using his hands for support. He had to run through a couple of backyards, jumped a few more fences as he made it safely back to the street safely.

He stepped onto Central Avenue out of breath, turned his jacket inside out and attempted to blend in with the crowd.

Rock tucked his jewelry underneath his shirt, trying hard not to draw any attention to himself. He stood with his back against the wall of a store, lighting up a fresh cigarette and started thinking about his next move.

He needed to get out of the city, then out of the State and ultimately out of the country.

Rock would rather die, than go back to prison.

His thoughts were interrupted by the sound of a horn blowing in the distance. He looked up to see a dark blue five series BMW, with tinted windows, double parked in front of him. The passenger side window rolled down halfway, revealing the silhouette of a male figure.

The driver leaned over to the passenger side window and said, "Yo Rock, that you cuz?"

The man named Sharif was brown-skinned with a wide round face and a thick Muslim-type beard.

"Do I know you cuz?" Rock asked with suspicion and distrust in his voice.

"Nah, but you know my peoples . . . you need a ride or something?" Sharif said.

Rock gripped the pistol underneath his jacket. The man looked kinda familiar to him, yet he wasn't sure who he was and wasn't about to take any chances.

Just as Rock had decided to send the stranger on his way, a squad car pulled up behind the BMW, flashing its overhead lights, then pulled off slowly, giving Sharif the evil eye as they crept by.

"Yeah fam, I think I will take that ride," Rock said, jumping into the car with caution, his hand still on his pistol, not knowing if someone was in the backseat waiting to ambush him or not, nor the intentions of the driver.

"What did you say your name was again?" he said.

"Sharif, cuz. I'm Reek's cousin," he said with a slight devilish grin on his brown face.

The first chance I get, Sharif thought to himself, *I'm going to rob this nigga, kill him and then dump his body in one of those trash bins in B.T., for killing my little cousin.* He pulled away from the curb with the evil grin still plastered to his face.

The mere mention of his best friend and crime partner Reek, had caused Rock to involuntarily shed a tear. As much as he would have like to hide it, his emotional display did not go unnoticed by Sharif.

He closed his eyes, relaxed in the seat and reminisced about when him and Reek had first met so many years ago.

Chapter 4

Reek was eleven, and Rock thirteen when they first met in their native Haze Homes projects. They had both been walking around aimlessly, searching for some food. By chance, they locked eyes on each other from across the parking lot.

It had been a record breaking 48 inches of snow that fell that morning and both him and Reek were outside with little more than thin ripped up leather jackets and holey corduroy jeans. They looked like the garbage can kids.

Both of their mothers shared crack addictions. Both have been in the habit of selling themselves to support their addictions. Everything went towards crack; welfare checks they received for their sons. Government issued cheese was even sold for crack. Truth be told, had it not been for the fact that Section 8 pays for their Public Housing or that too would have been up for sale.

Rock was cold, hungry and frustrated at the fact that he had to spend his childhood with the responsibilities of an adult. Rock stalked over to Reek in his tattered Pro-wing sneakers, "WHAT THE YOU LOKKIN AT?" he said, towering over the smaller, shorter Reek.

"YOU MA FUCKA!" Reek yelled, while poking his chest out, trying and failing to appear bigger.

"Don's make me cold cock you lil nigga," Rock said as he put his hands up and got into his fighting stance; the only thing his pops had taught him before he died.

Reek mimicked Rock's movements, putting his hands up and rocked awkwardly from side to side.

"What you going to fight or dance?" Rock asked him as he busted out in uncontrollable laughter.

"You a tough lil ma fucka... what's your name homey?"

"REEK!" he said, still rocking awkwardly from side to side with his hands up protecting his face.

"Come on Reek, you can chill with me," Rock said as he reached in and put his arm around Reek's shoulders, ignoring his funny fighting stance.

"First thing we have to do is teach you how to box," Rock said, then added as an afterthought, "By the way, my name is Rock."

The two young boys got acquainted with each other throughout the day. As the light turned black, the two boys witnessed as they did every night, sights and sounds of the ghetto.

There was an old ragged dope fiend woman giving a blow job to a local hustler's pit bull in one of the dark corners inside the project building.

The dog was panting and wagging its tail, as he laid on his back, being cheered on by a small group of hustlers and neighborhood fiends alike.

This was a nightly ritual for some of the more hardened criminals in the projects. Their cold moral-less hearts caused them to degrade female fiends in a way unbeknownst to humanity.

To them, fiends were nothing more than soul-less, mindless zombies.

Rock and Reek walked to the edge of their project building, trying to catch a better look at the shootout that was developing right before their very eyes.

"LOOK ROCK!" Reek screamed with excitement, as he pointed towards the action. A cop car was only a half of a block away from a black 5.0 Mustang.

As the Mustang rounded the corner, the passenger peeked half of his body out of the sun roof, shooting at the pursuing squad car with a Uzi machine gun.

This is a scene right out of a movie, Rock thought to himself as he watched the driver round the corner and throw something out of the window, then sped away up the block, creating even more distance between them and their pursuers.

"COME ON REEK!" Rock whispered, urging his new friend to follow him. "I THINK THEM NIGGA'S JUST TOSSED A BAG OF FOOD OUT THE WINDOW!" Rock said with excitement.

Reek's little eyes lit up at the thought of eating something. The two boys hadn't eaten at all that day. Rock and Reek cautiously approached the black bag. Their stomachs growled audibly, scaring off a cat that was also persistently pursuing its meal for the night.

Rock knelt down and unzipped the black duffle bag that was laying in the snow. "What is it?" Reek questioned impatiently. "Is it some food?"

"I don't know," Rock responded, not knowing what to make of the white powdered substance. "It looks like some type of flour or snow," Rock continued.

Hunger overpowered logic and in a rush to get some food into his stomach, Reek had pushed Rock out of the way, tripping over his own feet, falling headfirst into the bag.

"What is it?" Rock questioned, as Reek picked himself up and attempted, unsuccessfully to brush the white

37

substance out of his hair and face. "I feel weird," Reek said after several minutes. Rock looked at his boy intently. His eyes were opened very wide, and he began to shake. "What's wrong with you?"

"I don't know. My face feels all funny," Reek said as he sat down on the curb, unable to maintain his balance.

"Yo Reek, you look like my moms when she be getting high off that stuff."

"I feel real lightheaded," Reek responded, getting up, then falling back over in the snow, with a wide goofy grin on his face.

Rock walked over to the duffle bag and began to inspect its contents. He licked his fingertips, dipped them into the bag, then tested the powder. As he had seen other hustlers do before him, he opened his mouth widely, and took in a deep breath. He knew that if his tongue became numb, it was cocaine in the bag.

Once confirmed, Rock and Reek sold all of the cocaine they had.

Once it was time to re-up, they asked around at school and ran into a young Jamaican kid named Kya. Kya's uncle was a major cocaine supplier for most of West Orange.

When Kya had finally introduced them to his uncle, he immediately did not want to deal with them, referring to them as unreliable Yankee boys, but when Rock had revealed to him that not only was his father Jamaican, but one of the most rudest dudes in his day before he had passed away, the man had no other choice but to respect him.

When Rock placed his money on the table, Kya's uncle had called him to the back room. Kya then returned with a clear baggy filled with cocaine. "My uncle said you will deal with me only," Kya said with a Jamaican accent.

They exchanged money for product, then Kya added, "He said he is not going to deal with a pickney."

"What's that?" Rock and Reek said in unison.

"Oh, that pickney means young man," Kya instructed.

Rock and Reek had no other choice but to respect the rules to the game that Kya's uncle had put in place. Besides, Rock thought he would have preferred to deal with Kya anyway, especially when Kya had given them a nine-millimeter Beretta before they left.

"Here," he said. "Protect yourself; the game is rotten to the core."

Rock grabbed the gun and drugs, thanked him and never looked back. Him and Reek was on ever since.

"Yo Rock, where you want me to drive you to?" The sound of Sharif's voice had broke Rock out of his trance.

"Can I use your phone homey?" Rock asked, looking exhausted and out of it.

Sharif handed Rock his cellphone, feeling uneasy and confused on the subject of whether or not Rock was the one that had actually killed his little cousin.

He decided that Rock couldn't have killed him. Sharif had run into many killers in his day and have yet to meet one that had cried for their victims.

Sharif's plans had changed, and he now decided to see where this situation would take him. He knew that Rock and his cousin were making alot of money, and he hoped that Rock would be on the lookout for a new partner.

"I need you to take me to Elizabeth," Rock said, as he dialed the number to the house he sometimes shared with his girlfriend of ten years.

Chapter 5

Jacquie was on her knees, servicing her lover of the past three years, Michael, when the phone rang.

Michael was slouched down on the couch, with his head leaned back and mouth gaped open, enjoying the head he was receiving from another man's girl.

Sure Michael didn't have the riches that Rock did, or live with lavish lifestyle that Rock did, but he did have one advantage over him, and that was G.A.M.E.

He'd also had Rock's girlfriend on her knees, giving him the best blow job that he ever had. Her thick, moist lips, wildly roaming wet tongue, had him cumming down Jacquie's tight throat in seconds.

"AAHHH SHHITTTT, BABY!" he said, as he grabbed the back of her head and a hand full of her hair and power thrusted his small fat penis into her open wet mouth, making sure that she had swallowed every single drop of his semen.

"Michael you know I hate when you do that," Jacquie complained, as she got up off of her knees and dusted herself off.

At one point, when she was sucking on Michael's dick, she heard the phone ring. However, when she had attempted to answer it, Michael thrust his penis to the back of her small throat, then came in her mouth.

Jacquie didn't mind servicing her lover. In fact, she rather enjoyed it. However, what she didn't like was the fact that the only reason that Michael had insisted on cumming down her throat was because he knew that every time Jacquie kissed rock it was like kissing his dick.

Michael hated drug dealers. To him, drug dealers were lazy and didn't deserve the expensive lifestyle that they did, without having to lift a finger.

Besides the fact that Rock was paying for Jacquie to go to college, Michael didn't see any good in Rock and if he had his skinny little way, he would kill the little bastard himself and take Jacquie away forever.

Michael hated to admit it, but he had secretly fallen in love with her.

At first, he just wanted to fuck her and spend some of Rock's money in the process, but somewhere between that venture, he had fallen for her hard.

Sure Jacquie had been short and overweight, but what she lacked in height and weight, she made up for in sex appeal. Her hair was shoulder length, and though it was dark red it complimented her brown oval shaped face.

Her breasts were bouncy double D's and her hips were wide and proportionate with her stomach, even though it protruded slightly more than the average woman her age.

In remembering when he had first met her, in the parking lot of Rutgers University College three years ago.

Jacquie was driving a gray Chrysler M300, with big chrome rims and low profile tires. He remembered it like it was yesterday. He was driving his mother's old beat-up Ford station wagon. They had almost crashed into each other when they both tried to park in the same parking spot. Michael had backed off and allowed Jacquie to take the parking spot.

Michael, never one to miss out on an opportunity, suggested that if she really wanted to thank him, she would join him for dinner.

Jacquie was reluctant at first, however reasoned that if Rock could have a side woman or two, why couldn't she?

A couple of weeks later and they had been fucking like rabbits.

"RING ... RING ... RING ..." Jacquie ran to the phone so fast that her mini-skirt had flared up in the air, revealing her thick hips and chunky buttocks. She knew she had to get to the phone before Michael did.

Sure she did enjoy his company, however Jacquie wasn't no fool. She would never leave the security and comforts that her man provided.

She noted that Michael had been acting strange lately, as if he was trying to expose their secret love affair to Rock, a development that she hoped would never happen, knowing the outcome would be grim.

"Hello?" Jacquie said, while leaning over a nightstand, and resting the phone between her shoulder and ear.

"Baby, it's me."

"Hey Rock, how's my future husband doing?" she lied.

"I'm fucked up in the game right now boo," Rock answered, paused then continued. "I'm going to need you to pack a little bag and get ready to go on a little trip with me."

"Where we OHHHH ...," Jacquie responded, feeling something hard, fat and warm enter her pussy lips from behind.

"What's wrong?" Rock asked, sensing her distress.

"OHH ... nothing daddy ... I just now had this sharp pain in my lower back," as she attempted, but failed to maneuver her body away from Michael, who was now ramming her ass hard as his fat little dick would allow.

"OHHH GODD!" Jacquie screamed out while trying to cover her mouth, hoping that Rock didn't hear her.

Even though Michael wasn't working with much downstairs, he sure knew how to work what little he had, she thought to herself.

For most women it's not the size of the boat, but the motion in the ocean; so they claim.

"THAT'S RIGHT . . . TAKE THIS DICK!" Michael blurted out near Jacquie's ear, knowing that Rock would hear him.

"WHO THE FUCK IS THAT?" Rock asked as he sat straight up in his seat.

"Noooo . . . body daddy. I was just watching this porno movie," she lied.

Furious, Michael snatched the phone right out of Jacquie's hand and began to talk to Rock.

"IT'S ME NIGGA, POUNDING YOUR GIRL OUT ALL CRAZY OVER YOUR NIGHTSTAND!"

Rock was so upset that he couldn't even respond. All he was able to do was press the dial tone on the phone and hang up.

Rock didn't want to give the man the satisfaction of hearing him upset. Besides, Sharif was only minutes away from the house and Rock knew that the man had no way of escaping what he planned for him.

"What's wrong?" Sharif questioned, noticing the change in Rock's posture.

"Nothing," Rock mumbled, while thrusting the phone back into his hand.

"Something has to be wrong. What your chick leave you or something?" Sharif asked.

Rock didn't want to answer him. However, for some reason he knew that if he didn't, Sharif would have never dropped it.

Though he didn't really know Sharif, Rock could tell that he was the persistent type, so he decided to answer him.

"Yeah homey, my bitch cheating on me," Rock said through clenched teeth. "Make a right on Renner . . . and park up. We're here," Rock said, cutting Sharif off before he even had an opportunity to ask questions.

Sharif parked the car in front of a large two-family gray house. There was a time for talking and Sharif wisely decided that now was not the time.

Rock scooted up from the seat, then pulled the Tech-9 from out of his waistband. He wanted to check his weapon before he entered the house. Although the gun looked fairly clean, Rock knew that Tech's had a history of jamming and he didn't want anything to prevent him from exacting his revenge.

Sharif mimicked his movements, pulling his own weapon from its holster and inspecting the large Desert Eagle for flaws.

Rock took note of the gesture and said, "Good looking on the back up family, but what I really need for you to do is keep the engine running and be ready to help me get my work out the house . . . you heard?"

He jumped out of the car and slowly creeped up the steps. He carried his gun low.

Even though it was dark outside, he still didn't want to alert the neighbors to his plans and more importantly, Michael and Jacquie, to what was ready to jump off.

He slowly inserted his key into the front door. Surprisingly the door gave way, opening to the most horrific thing that Rock had ever imagined seeing. Rock rapidly squinted his eyes, trying desperately to blink away the carnage in which he was viewing. Never in a million years would he have thought his girlfriend of ten years would betray him like this.

Jacquie was butt naked on his living room floor, getting fucked doggie-style by a skinny, tall, light-skinned stranger. The stranger looked up at him, smiled, then went back to fucking his girlfriend as if he wasn't even standing there.

Rock couldn't believe his eyes. He felt disrespected, betrayed and heartbroken all at the same time.

It wasn't until Rock had completely crossed the threshold of the front door and revealed the Tech-9 that he had in his hand, that the stranger had the good sense to pull his dick out of his girl.

The sudden interruption of pleasure caused Jacquie to look up. "WHAT THE FUCK! WHY YOU STOP FUCKING DADDY?" she questioned. Michael never responded. Instead, he continued to look at Rock's gun with horror-stricken eyes. Jacquie finally followed his eyes and was surprised to see her boyfriend standing in the doorway with a Tech-9.

She stood up as quickly as she could, then ran her hands down her bare skin as if she was wearing clothes, in an off-handed attempt to appear dignified.

"ROCK BABY WE WASN'T DOING NOTH . . .," was all she was able to get out before all hell broke loose.

Michael had jumped up and seeing the gun in Rock's hand, spun around towards the back door and started to run in an attempt to escape.

"NO YOU DON'T," Rock yelled as he raised the barrel of his Tech-9, aimed and squeezed the trigger.

"TATTA, TAT, TAT!" was the last thing that Michael ever heard. He almost made it all the way to the back door, before he was cut down by the Tech-9's bullets.

The forces from semi-automatic sub-machine gunfire had caused him to lift and spin in the air like a ballerina on meth, then crash to the floor with a sickening thud. His head rested at the bottom corner of the back door, while the rest of his body was contorted in an awkward, chilling position.

From his waist up, he was laying towards the door, while his other half was doing something entirely different. The bottom half of his body was twisted towards the ceiling. Clearly the impact from the bullets and the way he landed, caused him to sever his spinal cord.

46

Although Michael's soul had long since left this earth, his body's nervous system remained, causing him to jerk and twitch, with his eyes still opened with an expression of horror on his face.

To the average onlooker, it would have reminded them of a scene straight out of a Stephen King movie, the way Michael laid gruesomely on the floor.

Rock stood there in a trance-like state. For the first time in his life he didn't really know what to do.

He had treated Jacquie like his queen and never suspected that one day he would be standing in the middle of his own front door, trembling after having shot his girlfriend's lover.

Tears involuntarily ran down his face as his mind seemed to distance itself from the stressful situation. From that moment on, everything seemed to develop in slow motion. he could see Jacquie crying and screaming. However, he couldn't hear her.

Rock watched helplessly as Sharif crept up behind Jacquie, pressed his Desert Eagle to the back of her head, then pulled the trigger. He had tried to warn her, but when he opened his mouth nothing came out.

It wasn't until the hammer of Sharif's gun made contact with the back of the bullet and Jacquie's forehead had exploded like a grapefruit, sending chunks of bone fragments, brain matter and blood splattering all over his face and clothing, that reality set in. His girlfriend of ten years had been killed.

Before he knew it, Rock had found himself again lifting up his Tech-9, taking aim and taking another man's life.

The three bullets had taken Sharif by surprise, hitting him in his upper chest and neck. Sharif laid first on his back, mumbling something as blood flowed freely from his mouth.

Rock walked over to him and bent down in an attempt to hear the dying man's last words. At least he owed him that much!

"That bitch was cheating on you dog . . . I . . . I thought you wanted her dead," Sharif managed to get out just before Rock put a bullet in his temple, ending his life.

Rock hated the fact that he allowed his emotions to get the better of him. Though he didn't know Sharif all that well, he regretted killing him, because he was his best friend's dead cousin and his heart actually was in the right place. However, it just wasn't shown at the right moment.

Rock ran to his bedroom, quickly he stripped down to his boxers, boots and pants, then tossed them in the corner of the room. He ran to his closet, opened the double-doors and began the task of dressing himself. He grabbed his black Polo jeans, wife-beater, white Tee, black scully and black leather jacket and dressed.

Rock then reached down to the corner of the closet and pressed a button. This button was so small and inconspicuous that the average person would never have noticed it unless they knew that it was there. Rock himself had to feel around the corner of his closet a few times before he was able to finally locate it.

He pressed the button and heard the sounds of his ten thousand dollar investment at work. Rock watched as the bed lifted and the hidden wooden floor panel underneath it slid back, revealing a digital floor safe.

He quickly punched in the numbers and opened the safe. Once inside, he unzipped the black duffle bag and began to inspect its contents. He went through the inventory in his head, "one-hundred thousand dollars, Beretta M468, Russian Tiger Body armor, two Smith & Wesson 500 handguns, keys, and his trusted Uzi with extra extended clips." Everything accounted for.

The Uzi was one of Rock's first and even though it was the oldest of the bunch, it had gotten him out of many jams and he just could not bring himself to get rid of it. He reasoned that if he ever found himself in a shootout or needed to get some nigga's up off of him, the Uzi was his favorite weapon of choice.

Rock also had three kilos of raw cocaine in his bag. The cocaine and the hundred thousand dollars had been what was left from him and Reek's last flip. Reek had been responsible for the other half of the product and money and Rock had no idea where he kept any of it.

The cocaine he had was pure and he was in the habit of turning three kilo's into five, just by stepping on it.

Rock mentally kicked himself in the ass at the thought of not being able to retire, because of what happened to Reek. He only had one more flip to go before he was able to exchange his money in Jamaica, but with living like a king, he needed Reek's help to accomplish his goal.

As in all wholesale businesses, the more you copped, the more you got and on this last flip his connect was going to give him and Reek the flip of a lifetime. At twelve thousand a kilo, Reek and Rock were going to purchase roughly fifty-five kilo's, with a wholesale value of about one-point three million dollars.

Rock made a mental note to get in touch with his connect Kya, once he got settled into his new location.

He grabbed his duffle bag and ran to the back door as quickly as his legs could carry him. His kitchen was located near the back door, so it wasn't hard to set his next plan into motion. He set his bag down, opened up the bottom of the oven door, then blew out the pilot light. He also blew out the pilot light on the top stove before turning all of the gas dials to high.

He then picked up his bag and forced the back door open. Rock had to jerk the door a couple of times before it gave way, because Michael's head and torso was in the way. He banged his head with the door, disrespecting the dead man's corpse numerous times before the door gave way.

Once outside, he lit up a fresh Newport that he had in his jacket pocket, took two deep pulls from it, then closed the door, leaving the lit cigarette crested between the door jamb and the closed door.

Though he'd never attempted it before, he reasoned that once the gas from the oven filled the room, the lit cigarette would ignite from the fumes in the kitchen, causing the entire house to explode and burn to the ground, leaving any evidence that the police could possibly use to arrest him, non-existent.

Rock then entered his broken down garage located in the backyard. He felt confident that his 2004, 911 Porsche Turbo would still be there, even in "Brick City," once dubbed the stolen car capital of the nation.

He opened up the tattered, creaky garage door. *Thank God his car was still there*, he thought to himself.

Rock looked over his black beauty with its limo tinted windows, black rims and run flat low profile GT pro-circuit racing tires.

He smiled, knowing that no one had ever suspected that such a immaculate automobile would be stored in such a broken down shack of a garage like this.

He jumped in his whip, then started it, content in the fact that it was untraceable to him. He knew he should not have any problems with the highway patrol, or niggas he had beef with, since he never drove it.

Yes, that particular car had only one purpose; that was to get him out of a sticky situation and as fast as humanly possible.

Rock switched his CD player on, as he crept down his long driveway, out onto the street. Sounds of 2PAC's N.I.G.G.A. song blaring out of his speakers.

As Rock looked onto his dashboard mounted rearview camera's he could see his plan manifest itself as he drove off. Simultaneously, the house exploded in an array of smoke and flames. The quiet Elizabeth block had been invaded by an explosion similar to a 4th of July celebration.

Rock, for the last time, glimpsed into the rearview and thought about the life he was leaving behind.

* * * * *

Lanceen was extremely exhausted when she pulled into the Shell gas station located in Norfolk, Virginia.

She'd been up for three days trying to find a lead on where her man Rock could have gone. She had been declared rogue by her supervisor, on top of which, she had found out that she was pregnant. Lanceen was totally convinced that Rock was the father. Besides, she had been three months pregnant and he was the only man she was sexing with at the time.

After days of pounding the streets, gathering intel on the computer, she'd finally found a lead. Lanceen had found out that Rock had some family in North Carolina and even though it was a long shot, she'd have to follow through on every lead possible if she was going to get the man responsible for her ruined figure.

Her thoughts were interrupted by a dirty middle-aged man attempting to wipe her driver's side window. No doubt a dope fiend trying to make a quick buck to get his next fix.

The awkward part about the whole situation was that even though it had been raining cats and dogs, the man was still outside trying to make a dollar.

Lanceen cracker her window and yelled at the man to stop. "No, it's no problem, ma'am. I'll have the windows spic and span in no time," the man said in a raspy voice as he ignored her and continued with the windows.

Lanceen rolled her windows down further and stuck her head slightly out. "Yo, I said I was good. Now get your fiend ass off my fucking car." The man stalked over to her open window feeling hurt and disrespected. How dare this uppity bitch disrespect him like that, after all the hard work he put in on her windows.

Yeah. It was raining and yeah he was truly a fiend, but she had no right to tell him about it. The man was enraged. He was out there all morning and hadn't made a dime and now this bitch was yelling at him.

That was the last straw. The man decided it was time that somebody learned a lesson.

The man raised his middle finger up at Lanceen and began screaming, "Bitch. First of all I was trying to get your dirty ass windows clean so your fucking dumb ass wouldn't have an accident. Second of all . . ." was all he had gotten out of his mouth before Lanceen pulled out her standard issue .40 caliber and placed the barrel of her hand cannon against his nose.

"WHAT'S THAT NIGGA?" Lanceen asked with a murderous glint in her eyes. The man had completely done a 360, stuttering out apology after apology in an attempt to save his own feeble life.

He started off with an excuse. "Ma'am I just wanted to wash your windows so you wouldn't crash your nice car. I was going to do it for free," he continued. Lanceen gestured with her gun for the man to get away from her car.

The man took the hint and walked away, mumbling the word "bitch," in his wake. "WHAT WAA THAT?"

"I said have a nice and blessed day beautiful," he said walking away with his head down. He knew that a lesson had been taught that day and unfortunately, he was the one who learned it.

Lanceen refueled her car without any further incident. She then walked into the store and grabbed a pickle, bag of nachos and a small ice cream for the road. She had a long way to travel before she would reach North Carolina and she figures that the pickle, ice cream and nachos would satisfy her cravings.

Chapter 6

Reek woke up in the basement of the New Essex county jail, aka, "THE GREEN EYED MONSTER." He would have been surrounded in complete darkness, had it not been for the semi-broken overhead track light that flickered off and on.

His cell looked like a scene from an old gangster movie. Every time the light would flicker on for a brief moment, Reek could see his filthy environment.

The walls of the cell looked a purplish, black color. No doubt from years of dirt, grime, blood, urine and feces. The cell contained no bed and the only furnishings were a sink, toilet and rusty old mirror.

"AAAHHH . . ." Reek winced in pain as he attempted to move off of the sticky floor. "WHAT THE FUCK," he yelled as he felt pain shoot all throughout his body, but mostly in his chest and ass area. He could vaguely remember being shot in the chest, but for the life of him he could not remember what injuries he sustained that was causing his ass to hurt so much.

Reek fought through the pain and after a few failed attempts, stumbled to his feet. The unknown pasty substance that had been laying on the floor for God know how long, was his primary reason for getting up. His secondary reason and just as important and fighting the pain was so he could reach the mirror and take inventory of his injuries.

Reek stumbled over to the mirror, holding his ass cheek in pain with every step. Looking in the mirror, he could see that he was wearing the same clothing the night he was shot. His t-shirt still contained the evidence of the .380 cal. slugs that ripped through his chest. He adjusted his shirt and put a finger through the holes, counting each bullet hole out loud and thanking God each time that he survived.

From what he could feel, his chest wounds had healed fairly well, which caused him to question how long he had been out of it—one week, two? It had to be months Reek reasoned, because he would not have healed this much in a matter of weeks.

The thought of him laying on that filthy floor for months angered him to the point that he smashed his fist and broke the glass mirror, slipped on a wet spot near the sink and fell hard, landing on his butt.

"AAAHHHH . . . SHIT," he screamed loudly. Curiosity and pain getting the better of him, Reek was no longer able to delay the inevitable, that somehow his ass had gotten injured.

He ran through a list of scenarios in his mind as he reached underneath himself and began the painstaking task of examining his rear end. "*Maybe when I was shot I landed on something,*" Reek thought to himself. After examining himself and finding a big gaping hole in his ass, the harsh reality finally set in that somebody had violated him. Reek was furious, so furious that before he knew it, he was at the gate of his cell, kicking and punching with no sense or regard for pain.

Reek's manhood had been violated and someone was going to pay with their lives. Reek's emotional outburst was starting to create a disturbance on the cell block.

It was 12:30 in the morning and most of the convicts had been asleep prior to Reek waking them up and it wasn't being taken lightly.

"AH SHIT, BUTTY BOY FINALLY RAISED OUT OF HIS THREE MONTHS OF SLEEP," one convict yelled jokingly.

"FUCK YOU," Reek countered.

"NO YOU THE ONE THAT GOT FUCKED," a short, fat redneck C.O. said as he stepped into Reek's view and smiled.

"I'M GOING TO KILL YOU MA-FUCKA," Reek whispered through clenched teeth.

"WHATEVER NIGGER," the guard countered as he walked away with an arrogant stride.

Reek was still very upset. However, he calmed down once the voice of his mentor and best friend chimed into his head. He remembered that Rock had once told him that, "ANGER HAD NO PLACE IN BUSINESS BECAUSE ANGER CAUSES A NIGGA TO MAKE MISTAKES AND MISTAKES ARE COSTLY."

Reek found a dry corner of the cell and sat there, legs folded Indian-style. As he had often seen Rock do when faced with a difficult situation, Reek closed his eyes, slowed his breathing and meditated on it. He knew that kicking and screaming would get him nowhere and if he wanted to make it home, exacting his revenge on those who violated him, he would have to play his role.

Reek reached deep inside of himself and through self-reason was able to find inner peace. At least that is what he was trying to portray.

By morning time he had become a brand new man. He was humble as his façade would allow him to be. After months of pretending, Reek had finally convinced the guards to let him out of his cell, allow him a phone call and even offered him a job. However, Reek declined, reasoning that he could not trust himself to be in a position to kill one of them and exact his revenge.

He knew that if he did that he would never see the light of day. The first phone call that he made was to his lawyer. Reek thanked God that Rock had made him invest in a prepaid lawyer, which meant that anytime he was to get, "KNOCKED OFF" his lawyer already had a retainer. When he explained the situation to his lawyer, he was furious and vowed to get him out within the next couple of days. Reek was charged with conspiracy to commit murder. However, the police had nothing on him.

Since he had been the victim of the shooting and his firearm was never fired, they had to let him go. His lawyer also argued after obtaining Discovery on the case, that none of the bullets found in the victims bodies matched Reek's gun. After threatening the county with a lawsuit for police brutality, Reek was released within 3 business days.

He had been relieved when he was called to pack up. So much relief that when he was called, he left everything in his cell and just walked out. It took them about 4 hours to process him out, so by the time he smelled freedom it was six o'clock a.m.

He was surprised when his friend and connect Kya came to pick him up in a drop top Bentley Coupe. Kya had always been flashy like that. In fact, the only time you didn't see him in an expensive car is when he was either picking up or dropping off.

He had long since taken over the family business. Before his uncle had died, he made sure to pass on his yardy connection to him. Ever since then Kya had been living the Gee's life that street nigga's could dream of.

"What's up my dude," Reek greeted him upon entering the luxury automobile. "I see you still doing it all crazy."

"OH DIS, DIS A SMALL TIG MY YOOT." He put the car in drive, then continued. "Wait you see my collection."

Reek laid back in the luxury seats and for the first time in months relaxed. "So how did you know I was knocked?"

"Mea keep me ears to D'streets," Kya replied, turning up the volume on some classic Bugu Bantum. "Now relax U self. D'Don gotch yew now."

Reek went to sleep listening to "Shoot to Kill," and when he woke up, Beeney Man was playing as they were pulling up to Kya's 1.3 million dollar mansion located in Wayne, New Jersey.

"Come on you," Kya said, motioning Reek into his luxurious pad. The mini mansion opened up into a larger than life living room, complete with crystal chandelier and spiral staircase.

Reek's eyes popped out of his head when he saw that Kya had a line of naked girls standing on the staircase, one girl for each step. "Me not care if yew choose dem all," Kya said, pointing towards the beautiful array of naked women.

The women were all exotic and different. Some of them were Latin with thick hips and wide asses, while others were slim Asian girls. Kya even took the liberty to throw in a couple of dark and brown-skinned girls from his native country. The only similarities that the women shared was their age. They were all young, between 18-22 and some even younger.

Kya was aware of Reek being violated by the Newark Police Department and decided that the best way to get a man back in shape besides revenge was pussy.

After getting Reek laid, Kya had planned on pairing him up with his longtime Haitian assassin, "Money." Even though she was a female, Kya reasoned that she sure knew how to kill a nigga or bitch.

Reek could smell the familiar aroma of exotic marijuana in the air, as Kya passed him the blunt. He took two strong pulls from it and attempted unsuccessfully to hold the potent smoke in. He let out a small cough, instead of the massive cough that was lodged in his throat, trying not to embarrass himself in front of the audience of women.

Reek passed the potent weed back to Kya, then proceeded up the steps, carefully examining each woman as he passed them. He was looking for a particular type of girl and after making his way mid-staircase, he found her, or rather them. Both of the women Reek selected were Latin. They both were tall and young, however this was where the similarities ended. One woman had long, curly blonde hair, high cheekbones and the other had short, red hair with a slim jaw line.

He gently grabbed both women by their hands, then guided them up the staircase. "Me house is yours," Reek heard Kya yell as he entered the last room on the second floor and shut the door.

When Reek finally left the room it was nighttime. Reek descended the long spiral staircase and stepped into the dining room. To his surprise, Kya and his two young daughters and son were all sitting at the massive dining room table awaiting their meals.

"Come set and eat." Kya waved Reek over to a seat near his own. There was a plate, and utensils. Kya also took the liberty to have his staff set up a place for Reek's two women when they decided to come down.

"How day treat yew?" Kya asked Reek, referring to the two beautiful women he provided him with.

"Oh, the girls, they do very well, thanks." Kya's young girls turned to each other and joined in mutual laughter.

Even though they were young, both girls knew what Reek was doing with the girls next to their room, in spite of the fact that their overprotective father attempted to shield them from it.

The girls had even snuck next door and took turns looking in the keyhole, witnessing Reek's freaky sex threesome.

They were given strict orders to stay in their room, lock the door and they followed them. The girls even fell asleep and it wasn't until they heard what sounded like someone trying to break through the wall using their head as a battering ram, that the girls got up to investigate.

Minutes into the meal the two women came to join them at the table. The women looked worn out and tired, yet they still retained their natural beauty. The non-stop sexual escapades that Reek put on the girls and it was apparent on their faces.

After dinner everyone turned in for the night. Kya informed Reek of his plans to pair him up with his Haitian assassin and exact the revenge that he knew Reek would cherish more than pussy.

Kya woke up before the crack of dawn. Though it was 4:30 in the morning, Kya knew that she would be up and expecting him. Kya never liked to admit it. Yes, he was considered by all Jamaicans in the states and some back home, a certified "Don Dotta." Even he was afraid of his female Haitian assassin, Money. In fact, Kya wouldn't have ever dealt with her had he not inherited the use of her service via his late great uncle.

Kya jumped into his black Chrysler 300M, wearing all black jeans, a leather coat, vest, sidearm and a pair of Puma sneakers. He was in the habit of driving his cheapest cars whenever he had to make a run to Money's part of town. Even tough Kya was well known for shooting a nigga, he was no dummy.

He knew that even Don's were shot and sometimes even killed and he was not taking any chances, so he made sure to wear his thickest chest-plated body armor.

By the time Kya arrived at the Callinaides, it was still dark and most of the people from that project complex were still asleep. The only people that were out at this time were the dope dealers and zombie-like fiends that frequented the area.

Kya approached the tall, worn project building; with each step he became more and more nervous. Thoughts of what possibly awaited him on the 15th floor caused his entire body to tremble in fear and for good reason. Monay was not joke.

Legend had it that she played a pivotal role in freeing the slaves back in her hometown of Haiti many decades ago. She was also crowned the voodoo princess of Haiti.

It was said that once her house was invaded by a squad of 50 angry white men armed to the teeth with the best weapons of that time. The men had broken into her house in the middle of the night and locked themselves in, intent on killing her. The Haitian men and women in the community were quoted as hearing screams that night, unlike any screams they have ever heard in their entire lives.

When morning came, witnesses said they saw Monay's entire house covered with the blood and body parts of the men. There wasn't a wall or corner in that house that wasn't either covered in blood or contained a different body part in it.

The most horrific thing about the entire story is that among all of the chaos, Monay was found unscathed in her kitchen robe, cooking breakfast as if nothing happened. Many odd stories like that one infested Haiti like a wild weed plant. Kya had known of all the stories and believed them to be true, which was the cause of all of his nervousness.

He took in a deep breath before raising his hand to knock on the door. "Come in my love," a raspy voice said on the other side. "The door's open." Kya pushed the door open and before entering her apartment he tried to locate her in the darkness.

Mini droplets of murky darkness played on his eyes as he squinted them in an attempt to locate her. A flash of light from the pipe Monay was smoking flashed in the corner of the living room, illuminating her. "You have nothing to fear my love, please come in and shut the door," she replied between puffs of smoke. "Turn on the lamp, if that would make you feel more comfortable."

"Me always comfortable around yew," Kya said.

The dim light illuminated Monay's raggedy face. Who knew how old she truly was. Legend had it that she left her native land of Haiti some time in the early 1900's, on a tattered one man raft. Others say Monay used her magic to teleport from Haiti to America.

Whatever the case may be, the fact remains that she was currently residing in the United States and was trouble for anybody on the receiving end of her services.

"So you want somebody killed?" Monay said as she threw a set of broken human hand bones onto the floor, looked at them intently, then repeated the process.

"Ye . . . Yes," Kyla stuttered. "But this time I just want yew, to pair up with a partner."

"Sorry love, that's just not in the bones," Monay replied.

Kya hated when she knew what he was going to say before he did. What he hated the most about her was her weird voodoo practices. Monay was in the habit of requesting certain forms of payment that were unusual at best. An example of which, there were times when she requested an exotic form of plant life that would only grow in a remote place in Brazil. Other times she would request normal things, like gold or silver.

This time she had something even more horrific in mind for payment. Her slit eyes were reminiscent of a snake. "So you want me to murder the cops who violated your friend, Reek, huh?"

Okay, it didn't take a voodoo princess to figure that one out, Kya reasoned. The report of the rape had been all over the news and in every paper, yet and still Kaya had the instinctive feeling that Monay never read any papers. Hell, she didn't even own a TV.

He imagined that she sat in that old rocking chair of hers and played with her human bones all day, like she was now. "So is it a deal?"

"Yes." Kya answered her too quickly. "Hold up, what choo want for payment?" he questioned, realizing his mistake.

"A contract has been formed and you have already agreed to the terms," she said, pointing two fingers at him as if planting some type of hex on him.

"Alright," Kya responded, then turned and got the hell out of there as fast as he could.

For some reason every time he was alone with Monay, Kya felt like he couldn't breathe. Maybe it was the mothballs in her closet or the potent smell of whatever she had been smoking in her pipe, but whatever it was Kya never liked it.

At times after visiting Monay, it took him days to shake off the uneasy feeling he picked up from her place. It was as if she had some kind of evil spirits trapped in there with her. Maybe her apartment was purgatory, and evil spirits were trapped in there, stuck in limbo between heaven and hell. By the time Kya stepped out of the building, the projects had come to life with activity.

There were hustlers, robbers, whores and thugs alike on either side of him. Kya felt as if he was the star in the middle of some kind of killer Soul Train line.

"You got a light?" one guy asked Kya as he passed by.

"Nah," Kya responded, then pulled out his pistol and let it dangle in his hand by his waistband.

Kya was no dummy. He knew that if he had given the man a light, the next thing he'd be giving him was his wallet.

"It's like that homey?" the man asked with bewildered eyes. Kya never responded. Instead he stayed focused on getting to his car.

"YO, YOU GONNA BACK OUT ON MY MAN?" he heard another guy yell over his shoulder.

Kya started walking faster to his car. *Just a few more feet*, he thought to himself. Suddenly, he felt an empty beer can hit him in the middle of his back.

He turned around to see the crowd of people walking quickly towards him. Kya surveyed the crowd and noticed that a good number of them had pulled out their guns.

"COME HERE, LET ME TALK TO YOU CUZ," one of the men asked just as Kya jumped into his car.

Chapter 7

Rock jumped out of his car in a state of exhaustion. He had been driving for 9 hours straight. Fearing that his cellphone was tapped, he had purchased a "Throw Away," phone on the road, called his aunt in North Carolina and asked about his twin cousins, Keith and Kevin.

Rock had discovered that his little cousins were still up to their old tricks. They were still in the game and had even gotten a small condo in Henderson. He had received the information and made his Aunt Putten promise him that she wouldn't tell them that he was coming over to stay with them for awhile.

He took in his surroundings, taking note of the condo complex, then the cars in the parking lot. Most of the vehicles were fairly new and what he considered to be mid-grade.

Apparently none of the residents were balling on his level, because his car was the most expensive one there. Rock detected motion out of the corner of his eye and followed the husky figure all the way to his sheriff's car. The sheriff noticed Rock eyeing him, even in the foggy mists of morning and acknowledged him with a smile and wave of the hand. Rock returned the gesture, not wanting to draw any type of suspicion his way.

All the other condo apartments were located topside of the vast parking area, however Keith and Kevin's condo was located on a downward slope of the parking lot. Rock had to descent a long row of steps, then walk a short distance down the walkway before entering the complex.

Damn, more stairs, he thought to himself as he ascended a short staircase to the first floor apartment.

He appreciated the fact that his cousin's section of the complex was pretty secluded from the rest of the condo's. The only thing he didn't like in the immediate area was the fact that one of the neighbors was a North Carolina sheriff.

Then again, Rock reasoned, rubbing his trimmed beard, what better place to hide than in plain sight?

Rock rapped on the door labeled 2C and heard an immediate answer. "Who is it?" a strong manly voice questioned.

Rock decided to fuck with them. "IT'S D.E.A. OPEN UP." Rock could hear the quick shuffling of feet on the other side of the door, followed by faint whispers. He placed his ear to the door and could tell that both his cousins were in residence along with another, a female's voice.

"Just a minute."

Rock felt it was time to end the job. "Yo, it's your cousin Rock, open up."

Keith opened the door with a look of utter relief on his face. The previous day they just went to Atlanta and picked up 10 pounds of weed, the biggest they managed so far.

"Man, you scared the shit out of me," he said, embracing his big cousin in a bear hug and at the same time inviting him in.

"Yo, Kev, Rena, it's cousin Rock." They walked into the weed smoke-filled living room, only to see Kevin and Rena attempting to stuff pounds of weed between the seats of a long beige couch.

They both were oblivious to the fact that Keith and Rock just walked into the room. Rock decided to continue

68

on with the joke and nudged his cousin in the ribs, prompting him to play along.

He motioned for Keith to stand behind Rena, then he pulled out his pistol and stood behind Kevin and counted down silently using his fingers. Once all of his fingers disappeared, Rock placed the nose of his gun on the back of Kevin's head and they both yelled, "FREEZE," at the top of their lungs.

"SHOOT ME BITCH," Kevin countered in a deep tone.

"Now is that any way to talk to your big cousin?" Rock said as he lowered his gun, helped his cousin to his feet, then embraced him in a hug.

"Yo, Keith, Kevin, why y'all crazy ass cousin come all up in here playing with guns and shit," Rena said in a loud, angry tone.

It wasn't that Rena didn't like Rock, because she did. It was the fact that she didn't like guns. In fact, she was terrified of them.

"Yo, cuz who this loudmouth dark-skinned beauty you got over here?" Rock questioned, now focusing all of his attention on Rena, letting his eyes freely roam over her slim body.

"My name is Rena and would you please stop undressing me with your eyes."

Rock had known that Rena liked him, because when he looked at her lusting after her feminine features, she never shied away. Instead, she just returned his lustful stare with one of her own. Even Keith and Kevin could notice the sparks developing between them, however, Rock had other plans.

Heartbroken, he was not ready to start up another relationship. Besides, he was on the run and needed to get his money out of the drugs he had and then get out of the country.

"Whatever, Shorty. I'm cool," he responded, then turned his attention back to his little cousins. "So this what y'all doing now, little pounds of weed and shit?"

Kevin turned on the defensive. "Little pounds of weed, nigga we got 10 pounds of weed that's gonna bring us stupid paper."

"What's stupid paper?" Rock questioned.

Sitting down on the couch next to Rena, "Sixteen thousand dollars," Keith chimed in, defending their hustle.

"Let me try some of that shit?" Rock asked while reaching over Rena and grabbing the lit blunt in the ashtray.

He sat back and inhaled it deeply. "That's not too bad."

"NOT TOO BAD. Boy this here best trees in Henderson," Rena said, grabbing the blunt from him and hitting it herself.

"Sixteen thousand, huh?" Rock sat up. "Now I'm going to assume that you guys work together." They nodded in agreement.

"This means that 16,000 split three ways is five thousand, three hundred and thirty three dollars a piece, give or take a dollar."

They were all shocked at how quickly Rock's mind worked. "That's about right," Keith chimed in breaking the silence.

"Plus, if we subtract the cost of the pick up, living expenses, food, etc. you guys are going to end up with roughly 3,400 a piece at the end of the day."

Rock looked each of them in the eyes and could see their brains processing the information. After a minute, their faces seemed to dim, the reality of a bad situation does that to you. With the math Rock had broken down to them, it gave them a sense of defeat as if they were never going to make it out of the hood.

Rock was preparing them for the hustle on the big stage and treated them like he did all those who had worked for him. He always lived by the philosophy that one should first be knocked down before you could build them back up.

Rock had known that being too cocky in the drug game could lead to costly mistakes, and this was one of the cockiest bunch he'd seen in a long time. He could sense in their eyes that they were content with what they had, and Rock knew that in order to get them to hustle for him, he had to first break them down even more by informing them of what little they really had.

"So what do you suggest we do, get a job or something?" Rena questioned, being the first one to crack.

"No, I suggest you turn it the fuck up," Rock said, taking the blunt back from Rena and hitting it again.

"And how we do that?"

Now Rock had the attention of Kevin and Keith. "The Columbians call it Cocahenna," Rock said, standing up for more of a dramatic effect.

"So, what are we to do with all this weed? Stop selling it?" Kevin asked.

"Hell, no," Rock replied. "This is a juggler's game. We need all the work we can get . . . By the way, how's the Diesel market out here?"

"It's decent, but them nigga's in Raleigh got that sewed up," Rena replied.

"Either them nigga's going to work with us or work for us. I doubt they want parts of the last option," Rock said, then raised his pistol in the air to emphasize his point.

"Would you please put that gun away, you're making me uncomfortable." Rena moved to the other side of the room, visibly shaken.

"Yo, not to change the subject, but this blunt gone. You jokers got more?" Rock said, putting his gun back in his waistband.

"Nah cuz that was our last one. We was just on our way out to get more." Kevin grabbed the keys off the kitchen table and told the others to come with him.

"Y'all go without me. I'm just going to hang out here, okay," Rena said while looking at Rock. Kevin was secretly in love with Rena since high school. They had all grown up together and yet Rena had never given him the chance with her. When he tried, she said she didn't see him like that and would always think of him like a brother.

It angered him that she seemed so easily willing now to give herself to a complete stranger. "Oh now you wanna stay here." Kevin looked at Rena intensely.

Rena yawned her reply, "Yah. I think I'm going to get some sleep. I don't know why y'all got me up so early for anyway."

"We're supposed to be going to Radio Shack to put the rims and systems in the car, remember?" Keith explained. He thought of adding the fact that the night before, she was all excited to put rims on the 97 Honda Civic they all shared, however decided against it, not wanting to blow up her spot with his cousin.

"Well, I don't know y'all going to do, but I'm about to take a bath and go to sleep," Rock said, heading towards the bathroom. Keith and Kevin walked out of the door without saying another word.

Rock surveyed the cramped bathroom and was happy to see that they had a deep bathtub. He quickly closed the drain and began to run hot water into it. Then Rock looked around for bath soap. He was surprised to see that his cousins had some of the same bath products he used at home.

They had Saint Ives bubble bath, Epsom salts, bath beads and they even had Green rubbing alcohol. For those of you who don't know, these bath products in conjunction with each other create a boilermaker of relaxation. In fact,

I wouldn't suggest you fall asleep in such a situation, fuck around and drown. Rock closed the door, jumped in the bathtub, then closed his eyes.

He often used the soothing bath whenever he needed to meditate on a new plan or whenever he needed to re-evaluate an old one, and at the moment he had an awful lot to meditate on.

Just as Rock closed his eyes, he heard a soft knock on the door. Before he could protest, Rena slowly opened it and stepped in.

"WHAT THE ..."

"Sorry Rock, I had to go bad," Rena said as she took down her jeans and panties, then sat on the toilet. Rock couldn't help, but le this eyes freely roam over her beautiful chocolate body.

Her feminine features had him in a trance. "Do you like what you see?" Rena wiped herself, then stood up and put her pussy mere inches from his face. Rock licked his lips and admired her hairy snatch.

"I'll take that as a yes," Rena said as she climbed out of her clothing. "You hungry?" she asked, placing one thick leg onto the edge of the tub, damn near putting her pussy in his mouth.

Rock didn't usually have sex with random women, but there was something about Rena's overwhelming confidence and charisma that he just couldn't deny. The fact that she was extremely cute and equipped with the body of an Olympic swimmer didn't hurt either.

"Why you doing this, you barely even know me?" Rock couldn't believe the words that had just came out of his mouth.

"Don't get me wrong, this is the first time I've ever come at a dude like this. It's just that I feel that we share some type of connection."

Rock couldn't deny that there was a connection between them that he felt the moment he laid eyes on her. However, he decided to ignore it, trying to stay focused on his business of getting out of the country.

"Besides, I live every day as if it's my last one and as you can see, when I want something I take it." Without any protest, Rock wrapped his arms around her thick hips and butt, hugging her for a moment. Though Rena wasn't aware of why he hugged her so tightly, she cradled his head in her arms and comforted him, gently rocking him back and forth.

Before Rock knew it, he was openly crying in the arms of a woman he barely knew. He cried for the death of his boy Reek, for his dead parents and for all of the victims of violence that had died because of the drug game. Though Rock had played a pivotal role in the violence of the streets, he never wanted this type of life for himself.

After his brief display of emotions, Rock was embarrassed. Here he was, one of the most ruthless drug dealers on the East Coast and he was now breaking down in front of a woman.

Rena guided him to her room, adjacent to the bathroom and gently laid him down on her bed. He could barely look at her, due to his embarrassment. "Look at me baby," Rena said softly, as she straddled him.

"I'm going to love all of that pain away." She kissed him slowly from forehead to chest. Then gently sucked on his nipples while massaging his penis to life.

She then guided his member into her awaiting wet pussy. Rena rode him like she was an expert horse jockey, bucking and twisting his dick inside herself. "That's it baby, take this pussy," Rena said, breathing heavily. "Fuck me baby, this is your pussy now," she continued, causing his dick to become even stiffer in her pussy.

Rock felt a connection with her at that moment, unlike he had ever felt with any woman. "Damn, you feel so good," he whispered to her as he massaged her subtle breast.

Suddenly Rena jumped off of him and bent over, seductively with her shoulders and arms pinned to the foot of the bed. "It's your turn daddy, take what's yours," she said, while grinding her round, soft ass in a circular motion. Without further prompting, Rock mounted her like a stallion, thrusting his thick 9-inch penis deeply into her sugar walls. "Ummmm . . . I can feel it in my stomach."

Rock moved his hips in a circular motion and thrust inside of Rena as hard as he could. Rena's whines seemed to make him pound even harder. "Ummmm . . . Baby, I'm cumming," Rena said as she met Rock's movements thrust for thrust.

"Shit, Ma, I'm cumming too." He could feel the walls of her wet pussy pulsate and contracting onto his penis as they both came, then collapsed on top of each other in a sea of sexual sweat and love.

The sound of talking coming from the living room had awakened Rock from his peaceful slumber. He was oblivious to the time and it wasn't until he looked out the window that he realized it was night.

"Damn, was I out that long." He looked at his watch. It was 11:30 p.m. "That must have been some banging ass pussy."

"I'll say baby," Rena retorted, while turning around and looking at him.

"So you finally up?"

"Yea, I've been up watching you walk around my room named," Rena said, coming over and playfully kissing him.

"So do you want me to join your personal nudist colony, or are you going to get my clothes?" Rock said lustfully.

"I don't know. I'm kinda enjoying the view," Rena replied, playfully pushing Rock off of her.

"Well then, in that case, you better have a big purse, because I'm charging by the hour," Rock said as he rotated his hips in front of her.

"Okay, that's enough of that. You about to start something so back up. I have to go to the bathroom." Rena stood up and put her housecoat and slippers on.

"Could you get my clothes out of there for me please?"

"I'll think about it," she responded as she walked out and closed the door behind her.

On her way to the bathroom she was confronted by Kevin. He was just standing there against the wall with a hurt expression on his face. He never said a word, but Rena could tell by his face he felt heartbroken and betrayed. She felt bad for him and tried to speak, but Kevin just put a hand up in protest and walked away.

Rena used the bathroom, then returned with Rock's clothes and jewelry in her hands. When she walked into the room, Rock was sitting up on the bed. "Is that what you wanted?" Rena questioned as she playfully threw the clothes on Rock's face.

Rock grabbed her by the hand and pulled her onto the bed beside him. Then he kissed her and placed his platinum chain around her neck. A tradition in New Jersey and New York that symbolized that she was now his girl. "Are you serious?" Rena asked him with tears threatening to overthrow her eyelids. Just like Rock, Rena had grown up dirt poor and had to fight for everything she had.

"Of course I'm serious." Rock gave her a hug. "I told you that your pussy was some snapper," Rock said jokingly.

"Boy, get off of me." She pushed him off of her and put a mock expression of pain on her face.

"But seriously Boo bear, I think we share a real connection and I'm really feeling you and I . . ." Rena cut him off with a French kiss that should have been outlawed in all 52 states. That night Rena and Rock made love and talked the whole time, getting to know each other's minds and bodies in ways that took most couples a lifetime to accomplish.

Rock told Rena his whole story up to what landed him in North Carolina. And Rena told Rock how she used to get raped by her stepfather when she was younger and how she had caught him sleeping one night drunk coming out of a bar and slit his throat in a dark alleyway.

She explained that her stepfather had so many enemies that the cops didn't know the first place to look for a suspect, so they just gave up and the case went cold.

The next morning Rock and Rena awoke bright and early, both aware of what had to be done. "Baby," Rock said while tossing his car keys to Rena. "I'm going to need you to go in my trunk and bring me my black bag out of there."

"Okay baby." Rena paused by the door and said, "Which car is yours?"

"Just hit the button on my key chain and you'll see," Rock replied with a devious smirk on his face. He had been really modest with her. When he explained about his financial situation, he wanted her to find out on her own how close he was from completely retiring from the game.

Rena went outside, then walked up the steps to the parking lot. The fog from the night before was still in full effect and she could barely see the cars in the massive parking lot. She pointed the key chain in the air and pressed the button.

To her surprise the car right next to her chirped twice, then flashed its fog lights. Had it not been for that little mechanism on Rock's keychain, she wouldn't have ever been able to find his car. The fog was so thick that she hadn't even noticed prior to pressing the button that the car she was looking for was right in front of her face.

"Damn, this boy is pushing a Porsche 911," she said to herself as she ran a hand across the sides of the immaculate black beauty. She then opened the trunk and retrieved Rock's black duffle bag. *This boy must have been getting some major paper to afford this car*, Rena thought to herself as she picked up the bag then dropped it.

The sheer weight of the bag surprised her. "Do you need a hand young lady?" she heard someone say behind her.

"Fuck no," Rena retorted, only to turn around to see a uniformed sheriff standing right behind her.

"Excuse me," the officer questioned with a frown on his white ashen face. Rena kicked herself in the ass for her first response, then attempted to clean it up. She knew that whatever Rock had in his bag wasn't legal.

"I mean no thank you officer, I should be able to mange it," Rena said in a ladylike voice.

"You're sure, it really wouldn't be a problem," the sheriff insisted.

Rena quickly picked up the heavy bag and swung it over her shoulders. "No thanks, I think I got it now." Rena began to walk away.

"Wait a minute miss," the sheriff stopped her dead in her tracks. She could feel her heart damn near ready to jump out of her chest.

Rena just knew that somehow the cop had known what was in the bag and at any moment he was going to bust her. She thought of running, then quickly decided against it, knowing that the cop had an unfair advantage over her because he had boots on and she was wearing her Mickey Mouse slippers.

She cursed herself for tying to look cute for a man that was about to get her twenty-five to life in a Federal penitentiary. She looked towards her window and could see Rock standing on the balcony, taking in the entire scene with a worried grim look on his face.

She could see that he was very distressed and concerned about what was going on between her and the sheriff. At that very moment Rena was sure that whatever he had in that bag was not legal. She could see her whole life flash before her eyes.

She could already imagine the disappointed looks plastered on the faces of her mother and grandmother upon receiving the news that their sweet little Rena wasn't so sweet after all. Her palms were sweating profusely, and she was beginning to visible shake. *Oh my God, I'm going to jail for sure now*, Rena thought to herself.

Chapter 8

"Yeah bra, I can't believe that nigga Rock stole my bitch."

"It's not that serious Kevin. I'm sure there is a good explanation . . .," Keith said.

"A good explanation for what, Rena coming out of her room half-naked?" Kevin countered, banging his fist on the dashboard.

"Be cool Kev, you don't even know if anything happened. Besides, Rena is not your girl."

Keith's words stung him deep. He couldn't believe that after all of his efforts, another man was going to have Rena.

"That might be true, she is not my girl, but you not going to tell me they wasn't fucking," Kevin retorted.

Keith waved at a couple of girls as he drove by, then turned his attention back to his twin brother. "Oh you talking about the clothes we found in the bathroom. That don't mean shit."

Keith knew that what he was saying was untrue, however unlike his brother he wanted to take his hustle to the next level. Kevin may have been content with a small condo and a Honda Civic, but he wasn't.

He knew that his big cousin Rock was moving work on a heavy level and he needed to make sure his brother wasn't going to fuck up his chances of hustling on the big stage.

"Look bra, let's just concentrate on giving this chick this pound of weed and maybe see if they got that new Rock Nottay C.D. at the mall," Keith said while Kevin lit up a blunt and took a long pull off of it.

"Who is this new chick anyway and why is she willing to pay 5 'Gees for a pound of mid-grade weed?"

"I don't really know her, but that white chick Cindy said she was cool."

Kevin rubbed his chin in deep thought, then passed the blunt to his brother. "Do you even know what this bitch look like?"

"She said she was brown-skinned and had a sexy body."

"Keith, do you know how many sex brown-skinned girls there is at the mall? How we going know which one is her?"

She said she was going to be wearing a all red mini-skirt with black Timbs and a black halter top."

Keith parked in the mall's huge parking lot, making sure to put the car close to the entrance just in case they had to make a quick getaway.

"Hold on Keith, ain't that the bitch Cindy right there?"

"Where at?" Keith asked, turning around in his seat trying to get a better look.

"Right there in that white GS-400?" Kevin pointed to the car parked a couple of rows behind them.

"Oh yeah I see them and who is that bad-ass bitch I see jumping out the driver side with her?"

"I don't know," Kevin said, jumping out of the car and adjusting his belt. "But I saw her first."

Keith had to jog a little bit before he caught up with his brother. "Yo, the bitch with Cindy look like she got a little gut."

"What you call a gut, I call a thick bitch. Besides, she mad pretty," Kevin said, licking his lips, lusting after her.

"What's up Cindy, I didn't know you was going to be here too," Keith said, stopping the women. Had it not been for him saying something, they would have walked right by them.

"Oh, I didn't even see you."

Cindy didn't seem to be herself to Keith. For some reason she seemed like she was nervous or something. He decided to break the silence when he realized that Cindy wasn't going to introduce them to her friend. "So, I guess you're the chick that want the smoke?"

"Yeah, this my friend Lance . . ." Cindy looked towards Lanceen as if she was looking for some type of approval. When none came she switched up. "Yeah, this my friend Miss L."

Kevin extended his hand towards Lanceen and she pumped it. He then softly kissed her hand. "Nice to meet you Miss L."

Lanceen couldn't help but notice how much Rock's twin cousin favored him. The only real difference she noticed between the pair was Rock looked older, more mature and distinguished than them. In fact, had they wore dreadlocks instead of short fades, Lanceen might have mistaken one of them for Rock.

"Nice to meet you to Mr . . ."

"Oh, Kevin and this is my twin brother Keith."

"Thanks Cindy. I'll see you back at the car." Cindy rolled out of there as if she was a robot controlled by Lanceen. She didn't even have the courtesy to say goodbye. Lanceen turned her attention back to the twins. "So I hear y'all got the best weed in North Carolina."

"You heard right." Keith kicked him.

"What he means is we don't actually sell weed. We smoke it, and sometimes we got some extra, so we'll sell it," Keith said, feeling uneasy about the entire situation.

"Well then I hope you have an extra pound laying around here somewhere," Lanceen said with a giggle, deciding to play along with his game.

"So you bring the 5 Gees?" Keith questioned.

"Right here in my purse." Lanceen patted her bag.

"Okay, give it to my brother. He'll go to the car, run through it real quick, then drop off the smoke."

Lanceen looked at Kevin. "He's cute and all, but I'm not about to give him 5 Gees and just expect him to come back."

Now it was Kevin's turn to talk. "Nah Ma, we wouldn't want you to do that."

"My brother is going to wait right here with you while I count the dough and when I'm finished, I'll drive up and drop that off to you."

"I still don't trust y'all," Lanceen said, clutching onto her bag.

"Listen me, take my phone and my brother. If I don't come back you can keep them both," Kevin said as he reached for the purse.

Lanceen handed it to him and watched him walk away. It wasn't that she didn't trust them, she knew that they were legitimate. She just wanted to test them and see if she could get information out of them. She decided to press Kevin's brother now that he was gone, but knew that Keith was a horse of a different color.

"So, y'all live around here?" She decided to start off with small talk. However, Lanceen was well aware of where they lived. She knew everything about them through Cindy. Lanceen had contacted the North Carolina F.B.I. and with the help of local D.E.A. was put onto Cindy, who in turn was associated with the twins.

All it had taken for Lanceen to get Cindy to flip was to threaten her with 50 years of Federal time, threaten to take away her two kids and Cindy was a snitch. If Cindy had known the laws at the time, she would know that the FEDS would never have given her 50 years for an ounce of weed and two grams of coke. She would also have known that Lanceen had no probable cause to pull her over in the first place, and everything obtained form an illegal search and seizure would be inadmissible under the fruits of a poisonous tree doctrine. Cindy was unaware of any of these things, so once she was pulled over and Lanceen came out of her car with the contraband, she started singing like a bird.

"Listen ma, no disrespect, but this is a drug deal, not a meet and greet." Keith's words stung Lanceen. Her suspicions were now confirmed. If she wanted to infiltrate Rock's future organization, she would not be able to do it through Keith. But his brother Kevin might be a different story.

"Sorry, I just wanted to make small talk while we waited." She put her head down, sad expression on her face. She looked up to see if her ploy had worked and instead she was greeted with a stone cold expressionless face. Lanceen couldn't believe it. Keith didn't respond or even look in her direction.

What the fuck was going on, Lanceen thought to herself. Normally guys would give her their left kidney whenever she did her sad face look. What the hell was wrong with this guy? *Maybe he is gay*, Lanceen thought, or maybe, not it couldn't be, but maybe it was her. She looked down and mentally went through her own personal inventory. Black Jimmy Choo high heels, beautiful oiled thick caramel legs, red baby phat mini-skirt, black baby phat halter . . . What the fuck?

I'm big as a house. I can't believe I'm showing this much, Lanceen thought to herself. This baby is really ruining my life and it's not even born yet.

At that very moment she felt her baby kick. It was a if the little motherfucker knew she was talking shit about him. She lightly punched her stomach in the vicinity of the attack. That should shut him up, Lanceen reasoned.

She smiled at the fact that the baby had stopped kicking and her counterattack worked. She looked up to see that Keith didn't miss a beat. She knew that he saw the entire war she just had with her miniature sworn enemy. He had a peculiar, confused look on his face.

"You all right?" Keith asked, looking down at her with a frown on his face.

Oh, you finally alive, you stone faced bastard. If it wasn't for the fact that Lanceen needed him to get to Rock, this drug deal would have been their last. Lanceen would have lured them to a secluded spot and killed them herself, after relieving them of their work of course.

If you so damn smart, how you don't know you're about to sell a pound of weed to a Federal Agent? That's what Lanceen wanted to say, however her training prevailed over her hormonal imbalance. So instead she said, "No, I'm fine. Thank you for asking." She rubbed her stomach. "I think I just got a little heartburn."

"In your stomach?" Keith asked.

This nigga was too perceptive. Lanceen took a mental note to either kill him later or make sure he's not around whenever she was.

"I mean that I have a little stomach ache."

"No, it's fine. None of my business if your preg . . ." Keith's words were interrupted by the approach of his twin brother in the Civic.

Kevin parked right in front of them, then jumped out and popped the trunk. "Cute little car," Lanceen said with a hint of sarcasm in her voice. Kevin came over to them and handed her a black garbage bag filled with weed. Lanceen quickly looked into, then closed it back up.

"Thanks, I'll get back in touch with y'all through Cindy if I need some more," she said walking away.

"Hold on beautiful." Kevin grabbed her by the arm. "What about my phone?" Lanceen's first thought was to jerk her arm away from him, however knowing that she had a better shot of getting to Rock if she played nice, she thought better of it.

"Oh, I'm sorry, I almost forgot." She smiled, then handed Kevin his phone back. "I hope you didn't mind that I programmed my number in it."

"I didn't mind. I'm actually glad you put your number in there . . . this way I don't have to torture Cindy for it," Kevin said slyly.

They both laughed, then parted ways. Once comfortable inside the Honda Civic, Keith began to protest Kevin having accepted Lanceen's phone number.

"Yo, bra I don't trust that bitch."

"Who?"

"Miss L. I think she okay, besides, she just gave us 5 grand for a pound of week," Kevin said.

"What's up with that white bitch Cindy?"

"Yeah, I know. She was acting all weird," Kevin added in. "Yeah, that bitch didn't even say goodbye, and she owes me ten dollars," Kevin said as he started texting while driving. "Well we can forget that debt with the five grand sale she just hooked us up with." They both laughed in joy with that last statement.

"Here bitch." Lanceen tossed the pound of weed onto Cindy's lap. "You're going to sell every gram of this shit and get my money back."

Cindy was scared of Lanceen, but somehow still found the courage to speak out. "I thought you was F.B.I. They don't sell drugs?"

Lanceen pulled out a small .380 pistol from her inner thigh strap, then slammed it on the dashboard. "That's right, we don't sell drugs. However since I used my own pockets for buy money, guess what, you now work for me."

Cindy was now visibly shaking. The only thing she could see was the gun on Lanceen's dashboard.

She imagined if an F.B.I. agent wanted her dead, no one would be the wiser. While Lanceen looked cute and somewhat cuddly, so did bears and Cindy didn't have the urge to pet neither one. "How long do you want me to sell weed for you?" Cindy asked.

Lanceen never answered her question. She just put her car in drive and relished in the fact that she had instilled so much fear into Cindy, that she could make her do anything. She wondered how far she could push her before she toppled over the edge. Lanceen wasn't satisfied with just an ounce of weed, two grams of coke and Cindy's kids to hold over her head, she needed more leverage.

She needed some type of deep dark secret to keep this bitch completely in line.

"We going to my hotel to bag this shit up," Lanceen said as if she was the only person in the car. She looked down and saw that Cindy had put the pound of weed on the floor between her legs and for the first time noticed Cindy was damn near naked.

She involuntarily licked her lips at the sight of the young girl's slim, creamy white legs. The small skirt the girl had on had risen up since first entering the car, exposing her flawless legs and thighs.

Lanceen walked her eyes up Cindy's creamy body. She was short, petite, with long straight blond hair that overlapped her small C cup breasts. She could see that the girl was fearful of her and planned on using that to her advantage. Lanceen placed a hand on Cindy's 19-year old, trembling inner thigh, a little bit closer to her vaginal area than Cindy would have liked. Cindy trembled even more.

"Everything is going to be all right Cindy. I'm going to take good care of you," Lanceen said, all the while caressing her leg. Lanceen wasn't particularly interested in women, however the way her hormones were raging due to her pregnancy, she was now starting to consider the idea.

Lanceen thought, *what better secret could a straight woman have than sleeping with and working for a female Federal Agent.*

Cindy was starting to feel really uncomfortable. Lanceen went from stroking her legs and thighs to actually rubbing on her clit. Cindy found herself starting to get wet underneath Lanceen's touch, even though she didn't want to.

Cindy was too scared to protest Lanceen's invasion of her private parts and too nervous to enjoy it. She could never really enjoy another woman's touch, because she only liked men, right?

"Looks like were here sweetheart," Lanceen said as she removed her hand from Cindy's soaking wet crotch, then licked it clean. "Bring that bag wit you," she said as both women exited the car, then went upstairs to Lanceen's hotel room.

The room was hot and cramped. It had one queen size bed sitting in the middle of the floor. It was bare and had it not been for the bedside nightstand, lamp and dresser, the room would have been virtually empty.

Lanceen closed and locked the door behind her, then opened up one of the dresser drawers, pulled out a bag filled with empty packaging material and tossed it onto the dresser. "Get to work," Lanceen said.

"Could I go, go . . . to the bathroom, please?" Cindy asked nervously.

"Yeah sure, it's right there, but hurry up, we got business to take care of," Lanceen said as she licked her lips.

Cindy ran into the bathroom, closed the door, locking it. She was so scared and nervous that every bone in her body trembled. Her heart beat so fast she felt like she just completed a 20K long distance run. She sat on the toilet and began to pee. It felt good to finally relieve herself. She hoped that Lanceen didn't plan on raping her.

"HURRY UP IN THERE!" The sound of Lanceen screaming through the door startled the already frightened girl and caused her to jump off of the toilet seat, almost hitting her head on the ceiling. Lanceen was growing impatient with Cindy. This bitch was taking too long and Lanceen was beginning to lose her courage.

Truth be told, Lanceen was just as nervous as she was, though she was an expert at concealing it.

While Cindy was in the other room, Lanceen was pacing back and forth in the bedroom talking to herself. Finally she decided to calm down, strip down to her bra and panties, and lay on the bed. Cindy came out only to see the F.B.I. agent half-naked relaxing on the bed. Their eyes locked for a brief moment before Cindy ran to the dresser and started working on the weed.

Lanceen just laid on the bed and lustfully watched Cindy's slim hips sway back and forth as she bagged up the weed. Cindy could feel Lanceen's eyes glued to her soft supple ass, but still tried to relax as much as she could and complete the task at hand. Maybe she'll let me go home for a little while when I'm done, she reasoned.

Cindy almost jumped out of her skin when she felt a soft warm hand rub up her leg and caress her ass.

"I don't think you should . . . should be doing that," she managed to say, suddenly feeling faint.

Lanceen ignored her, brushed her long blond hair away from her neck, then began softly kissing her. Cindy was horrified, yet turned on at the same time. Like Lanceen, she had never even dreamed of being with another woman. Both women were breathing heavily.

Lanceen went from caressing Cindy's ass to rubbing her inner thighs underneath her skirt. Lanceen then pulled her pink panties to the side and inserted one, then two fingers inside of her soaking wet pussy.

"Na... na, no Miss Lanceen plea... please," Cindy managed to stutter out in a half-hearted attempt to squirm away from Lanceen's pleasurable touch. Though the feeling of her fingers inside of her felt good, Cindy never wanted to be with another woman in that way and knew in her heart of hearts that what was happening between them was far from consensual.

But what was she to do? Lanceen was a decorated Federal Agent and she—well she was nothing more than a young dumb country white girl from North Carolina. Who would believe her word over the word of a F.B.I. Agent?

Cindy managed to jerk herself free from Lanceen, only to trip and land face first on the bed. The impact caused her skirt to flair up and fold over her back, causing her soft, creamy cakes to be exposed. Lanceen felt like a wild animal, when just a little while ago she was undecided. Now her mind was made up and she really wanted Cindy.

Lanceen grabbed her by her legs and pulled them roughly, causing Cindy to crash flat on her stomach. She mounted her from behind, straddling her buns and pinning her down.

Lanceen then bent over and whispered softly into her right ear, "Cindy, I'm not going to hurt you, okay?"

"Ummm Hummm," Cindy responded with her face submerged in the pillow.

"This is going to happen, so you might as well relax and enjoy it." Cindy decided to attempt to take her advice. However, she still was unable to stop shaking. Lanceen was bigger and stronger than she was and she knew that she had no chance of overpowering her. Yet Cindy still couldn't believe she was about to get raped by a woman.

In all of her 19 years, she never imagined this type of fate for herself. Lanceen kissed her neck softly, whipping her tongue back and forth.

Cindy's body jumped in response. "Shhhhh... I got you, just relax," Lanceen said in a calm soothing voice. She then traced Cindy's spinal cord down to the curve of her ass with her wet tongue, all the while softly caressing the side of her body. Cindy had to admit she actually enjoyed what was happening.

The only thing she thought truly stopped her from really enjoying the experience was the fact that it was being pleasured by a woman.

The next sensation she felt almost caused her to jump out of her skin. *Ohhh my God is that her tongue,* Cindy thought to herself. A passionate moan escaped her mouth before she could catch it. Lanceen had spread her ass cheeks and rotated her warm, wet tongue around the rim of Cindy's rectum—a shark circling its prey.

Then she struck, plunging her tongue into her asshole, exploring her inner anal cavity.

Lanceen's pleasurable attack on her ass almost caused Cindy to pass out from pure ecstasy. She'd never know that her anal cavity was capable of producing such pleasure. Before now, she had never allowed any man, or woman to explore her body like that.

"Ummmmm... Lanceen why you doing this to me?" she found herself asking. Before she knew it, she was totally living in the moment. Cindy had involuntarily started bucking her ass up and down, and side to side on Lanceen's probing slippery tongue.

The overwhelming delight that Lanceen's tongue was giving her, caused her to temporarily forget she was with another woman.

I'm turning this bitch out, Lanceen thought to herself. "Turn around sweetheart and let me taste that pussy!"

Without hesitation, Cindy did what she was told, removing her panties and opening her legs wide for Lanceen. She couldn't believe what she was doing. It was as if the normal Cindy checked out and the freaky Cindy took over. Cindy closed her eyes and awaited Lanceen's tongue.

She didn't have to wait long because in a blink, Lanceen was sucking on her exposed clitoris like a candy apple.

"Ummmmm . . . Lanceen, eat this pussy."

She grabbed a handful of her hair and gyrated her hot pussy in and out of her mouth. A few seconds later, and Cindy found herself having multiple orgasms. Her pussy juices overflowed in a waterfall of ecstasy. Lanceen removed her inner thigh weapon, then placed it on the nightstand next to the bed. She laid down next to Cindy, while removing her bra and panties. She nudged her, "Baby, it's my turn now."

Cindy couldn't believe her ears. Surely Lanceen didn't expect her to eat her pussy? She opened her gray eyes, looking towards Lanceen with a confused look on her face. The look of confusion from Cindy didn't go unnoticed by Lanceen.

She felt betrayed in a sense. Here she was giving this girl the time of her life and she acted as if she was too good to return the favor. This infuriated her and she decided if Cindy wasn't going to eat her pussy willingly, she was going to do it unwillingly.

Lanceen straddled her, then smacked her hard across the face. The blow left a red handprint on Cindy's porcelain skin. She was now more scared than ever. She began to beg and plead with Lanceen not to force her to have sex with her. However, the more she pleaded, the angrier Lanceen became. Finally Lanceen jumped on her face, then jammed her exposed clit onto her mouth. She then grinded her pussy down onto Cindy's lips.

"Stick out your tongue bitch, and do it right or so help me God I'm going to beat your ass all night!" Lanceen said, as she continued to rick back and forth over Cindy's opened mouth.

"That's right, eat this pussy," Lanceen moaned. Lanceen never knew how intoxicating it was to have complete power over another human being and how much that power would turn her on. The more Cindy struggled, the more Lanceen was turned on. Cindy was not enjoying one bit of having Lanceen's pulsating pussy thrust into her mouth.

She could barely breathe and when Lanceen finally exploded, the juices from her pussy were so overwhelming that it clogged up her nose and mouth, almost causing her to suffocate.

After minutes of violating Cindy, Lanceen rolled over exhausted and went to sleep. When she woke up it was night and Cindy was sitting over top of her crying hysterically. She had her own gun pointed towards her head. Lanceen lunged for the weapon and the sound of a single shot shattered the quiet Carolina night.

Chapter 9

Kya stepped on the gas pedal and sped out of the complex as fast as his 300 M would take him. He was appalled that the people from the colonnades disrespected him, the undisputed Don Dotta. At the same time he was happy that he made it out of there with his life. This has never happened to him before. Yeah, people would look hard at him, but they never actually attacked him before.

This had been the first incident. In any event, he vowed to make sure that it never happened again. Kya thought about calling Monay, however forgot that she didn't have a phone. He noticed that Monay was afraid of technology and that was all she was afraid of, so it seemed. He imagined that if he ever had a problem with her, he would pull out his cellphone, light up the screen saver, and play one of his ringtones and she'd probably have a heart attack.

He chuckled out loud at his own humor, thinking how a woman who had killed more than her share of people, could be frightened by something as small as a cellphone.

He then relaxed somewhat, turned on some reggae music, then began thinking about his longtime friend, Rock. He wondered where he was, if he was okay and more importantly, when he was going to get in touch with him for his next flip.

He also thought about Rock's last words before he went on the run. Rock had been so excited when he told him about having only one more flip before he could retire from the game. They even made plans to meet up from time to time in Jamaica.

His last thought saddened him, knowing that his longtime friend may never have the chance to accomplish his dream of retiring from the game permanently. Kya pulled into the safety of his gated mini mansion. To his surprise Reek was sitting on his steps with his head in his hands when he pulled up.

He jumped out of the car and approached him. "What's wrong my yute?" Reek picked up his head, unsuccessfully attempting a half-hearted smile.

"Nothing, I'm just worried about Rock." Kya had known that Reek was lying, however he decided to play along with him.

"Yah, me worry too." Kya considered the real reason Reek was feeling bad was because what happened to him in jail.

"So dat situation wit bobby lion is done." He put an arm around his shoulder. "Me a take care dat."

"I wanted to take care of them nigga's myself," Reek protested.

"Calm down, I'm sure Monay plan to do dat too." That seemed to cheer him up, because after that Reek asked Kya to drive him to his house in Livingston, so he could prepare to collect his back pay from his runners.

Kya dropped Reek off at his house, and Reek immediately went to work. He went to his bedroom upstairs, changed clothes, grabbed his trusty .45, then tapped his chest, making sure the vest that Rock had gave him for his 28th birthday was securely in place. With that, Reek headed out the door, not bothering to take any money with him, knowing that he would collect, once he was back out on the streets.

He hit the start button on his new rimmed up Cadillac truck, jumped in and proceeded towards the city to get his paper. While driving, Reek decided to check his gun once more, knowing that the job of collecting his money may require the use of it. He smiled at his last thought, thinking about how many nigga's he had to pistol whip with this very same weapon.

He was kinda surprised the weapon had survived, knowing how hard-headed nigga's was. He decided to go to Hawthorne Avenue first. He knew that his runners would be out there, even in the early hours of the morning.

As soon as he arrived and parked, a team of hustlers approached his truck and started emptying out their pockets, tossing bundles of money onto the passenger seat.

"Who got some weed on them?" Reek asked the crowd of hustlers.

"I do," a young, short brown-skinned teen said, eager to please his boss.

"Okay then, jump in Peewee."

The teen jumped in the truck, happy to be in the passenger side of such a plush vehicle.

""So you just going to put your ass all over my paper?" Reek asked with a serious look, but a joking heart. The young teen had been so excited to be riding with his boss, that he didn't realize his mistake until it was too late.

"I'm sorry, I didn't even see . . ."

"That's okay." Reek smiled, then stuffed the money in his pockets after the youngster handed it to him.

He pulled away from the curb, promising the other young hustlers he would return with more product for them to sell. All of the people who hustled for Reek were happy. They were happy because of the way him and Rock stepped on their product, so in turn he was able to pay off all of his hustlers with the extra paper from the step. So for every two kilos they sold for him, he would give them the third for free. Him and Rock had taken the drug game in Newark to a whole new level.

They knew that no one would dark attempt to short them, when they paid their workers better than the competition.

This form of hustling also ensured loyalty from his runners. Reek knew for sure that he wouldn't have any trouble collecting the rest of his money. However, he felt more comfortable riding with a passenger.

"We going to the dewdrop, lil nigga. Light that weed up," Reek said as he passed the teen his lighter, leaned back in his seat, flipping on some old-school Scarface music.

Reek slowly drove by the dewdrop, making sure to peep the entire scene. As he passed he noticed the normal group of hustlers that worked the corner. Some of them were his workers, others just regular people who were happy to participate in the free enterprise the game provided. A few houses down the street, Reek noticed another group of men standing awkwardly around somebody's front yard. He reasoned that had it not been for the fact that all of them were wearing black and stood up when they peeped his truck coming, he might not of noticed them at all.

Reek looked at the men with slit eyes through the safety of his dark tinted windows.

"Yo peewee, you see that gray house right next to them dudes over there?" Reek pointed to a gray rundown building that looked like it was abandoned.

"Yah," he responded, focusing on the building.

"I'm going to need you to go get my gwop outta there. Can you handle that?" Reek asked as he parked on the corner of the block, down the street from the house.

"Yah I can handle that," Peewee said, poking his chest out, trying to appear bigger than he actually was.

"You got a gun on you?" Reek asked, already aware of the answer. Peewee pretended to check himself as if looking for the gun that he didn't have. It wasn't that Peewee had never saw a gun before. Every hustler he knew had one. It was just that he never had the chance to get one.

Since he was only 14, pretending to be 16, nobody in the neighborhood wanted to sell him a gun. Regardless of this, Peewee still didn't want to appear weak in front of his boss by not owning a gun, especially at a critical moment like this. He was on the verge of earning a promotion.

Peewee was fairly new to the game, but he knew enough about it to realize that he was on the lowest level—a lookout.

A lookout was the lowest of the low, because at times they took the most punishment for the least amount of pay. A lookout only received $45 for a day's work, which was a small price for having to watch the hustlers backs for the police.

Not only did he have to yell "88" when the cops came, but he also had to be a decoy whenever the police ran down. Sometimes the cops, whenever he was caught, would just search him, then let him go, but come of the more seasoned professionals were hip to the game. After searching him and finding nothing, would beat him to a pulp.

He reasoned that after spending a couple of nights in a hospital with a thousand dollar bill for treatment, $45 just wasn't enough.

Being in the game for a short amount of time, he was always on the lookout for a promotion. And this was his chance.

"Here Peewee, take this." He handed him his back up .380 from under the seat, then continued, "Today is your lucky day Peewee. Yo ass a caseworker now."

Peewee could hardly conceal his excitement as he fumbled with the gun, awkwardly trying to find a place to put it.

"Here." Reek grabbed the gun. "Life up and turn around." Reek lifted up the back of the teen's jacket, stuffing the gun in his jeans. "Now you're ready."

Peewee turned around looking at him with a smile. "Thanks."

"Now I want you to go to apartment 3-D and ask for Big Nick and when he comes to the door, tell him I'm outside and to give you the bag. If he don't believe you, tell him to look out the window and I'll give him the nod."

"GOT IT," Peewee said as he exited the truck and made his way up the street.

"I'll keep an eye out for you," Reek said after Peewee jumped out. Reek felt bad he just sent the little soldier into a war zone, however he thought he should be all right anyway. Them dudes all dressed in black wasn't really paying them any attention anyway.

He adjusted his rearview mirror and watched Peewee with worry in his eyes, his hand resting on his .45.

Peewee was so excited to have been promoted to caseworker that he never noticed the hard looks from the group of men as he walked past them and into the 3-story building.

Reek, on the other hand, had noticed the entire situation, because he was already heading out of his truck, gun in hand, as soon as they followed Peewee into the building.

It was dark and creepy in the building. With every step that Peewee climbed, the steps creaked, revealing the building's deterioration. He began having second thoughts about this promotion, however felt Reek was not only his boss, but his friend and would never put him in a bad situation. With that in mind, he pushed on upward until he reached his destination, 3-D. He rapped on the door, hearing a deep male voice on the other side. The men who followed him were halfway up the 3rd floor landing, waiting for the chance to make their move.

Four of them, well prepared, weapons drawn, just waiting for the door to pop open, so they could spring into action and claim their bounty.

They had been scoping this apartment out for at least a week, watching load after load of fiena come and go. They guesstimated that they would take down a minimum of 60 thousand and change from this stick-up and even hoped they would take casualties, which would leave even more money and crack to split up between the remaining members.

These men were desperate, and itching to get high. On the other side of the door, Big Nick was happy Reek had finally showed up to collect his paper and hopefully drop him off some more product. He had ran out of crack two days ago and was really tired of sending his customers up the street to cop from the competition. Plus his baby's mother had been nagging him all day about buying some milk for their newborn baby Tariq.

Seeing Reek pull up in his big Cadillac Escalade made his day.

"Uncle Mike, sit your fein ass down, you don't answer doors round here," Big Nick said to his baby mom's fiened out uncle.

He hated he had to hustle drugs out of his baby mom's old apartment, especially with his son there, but he felt like he had no other choice. Where else could he conduct business? He could hustle on the street corner, but he wasn't from Central Avenue, so he knew that as soon as he stepped foot on the block he would have got himself killed.

To Nick, this was the safest place to hustle. Besides, his uncle was a local, so if anything they had to go through him before they got to him, since Tiesha's uncle was the one running all the customers.

"STOP TALKING TO MY UNCLE LIKE THAT!" Teisha yelled as she cradled her newborn son in her arms, breast feeding him breakfast. "And you going to buy me some new titties if this little monster of yours sucks my titties dry, since you can't buy no milk."

"SHUT THE FUCK UP TIESHA. DON'T YOU SEE I'M BUSY?" A pause. "Who is it?" Nick said as he pulled out his .25 and looked through the peephole.

"It's Peewee. Reek sent me to get that." It was dark in the hallway, however he still recognized Peewee as the young boy that jumped out of Reek's truck.

"Just a minute." Nick turned towards Teisha and with a frown on his jet black face whispered through clenched teeth, "Bitch, can't you do that shit somewhere else?"

"I wouldn't be doing this in the first place if somebody would buy some damn milk," Tiesha mumbled as she took her baby and went into the bedroom and sat down on the bed, making sure to leave the door open so she could be nosy.

Nick turned his attention back to the door and opened it without hesitation. "Come on in. What you say your name was?" Before Peewee could answer him, he felt a hard blow to the side of his head, then felt somebody push him through the door with such force that it caused him to crash into Big Nick.

Peewee crashed to the carpet, barely conscious. Big Nick was caught off guard. The intruders filled the room in a matter of second. Off balance and outgunned, Nick quickly threw his gun to the floor. He knew his newborn son and baby mom were in the back room and the last thing he wanted was a fire fight. Nick attempted to help Peewee up.

"Leave that nigga on the floor," said the leader of the masked man, pointing his gun directly at Nick's head. Nick dropped Peewee and stood up to address the robbers.

"What is this?"

The leader turned to one of his comrades and laughed. "What the fuck it look like nigga. It's a robbery!"

He then motioned for the others to search the apartment. They returned with a shaken up Tiesha and baby Tariq.

One of the intruders snatched the baby out of Tiesha's arms. She began to protest, however wisely decided against it, when another attacker violently smacked her on the side of her mouth with his gun. "That's it," Tiesha's uncle said, pulling out a long kitchen knife he had hidden under the couch.

"That was the last straw," the scrawny uncle said, standing up wielding the knife wildly. Thinking of the safety of his baby, Nick sprung into action. He wrestled the knife to the floor then smacked Tiesha's uncle so hard that he crashed onto the couch unconscious.

I've always wanted to do that, he thought to himself.

"OKAY, NO MORE FUCKING AROUND!" The gunman put the pistol to baby Tariq's little head. "NOW GO GET MY MONEY!"

Nick was visibly upset. The large muscles in his chest and arms tensed up. He knew he had to do something, then he remembered his spare gun he kept in the room under the mattress along with his money.

He looked over the gunmen, thought though they were all wearing masks, their body language told their story. They were anxious and fidgety, which told Nick that they were drug addicts. He stepped over Peewee and noticed he finally seemed to be coming around. Nick quickly went to his room, pulled the money from under his bed, then looked over his shoulder. To his surprise none of the men were paying him any attention. He quietly unzipped the bag and slid his hand under the mattress and retrieved his 6 shot .32, placing the gun in the bag and waling out of the room.

He again took in the room making sure to make a mental note of where everybody was located. Out of the corner of his eye, he saw movement in the hallway. He glimpsed that way and saw it was Reek trying to signal him with his hands, but he couldn't make out what he was trying to say.

"HURRY UP WITH THAT DOW!" the man holding his baby yelled. Nick then went into the bag and started dumping bundles of 50 and 100 stacks into the man's hands nearest to holding his baby.

The gunman had to put the infant on the floor in order to catch all the money that was being thrusted into his hands. The others were transfixed on all the money that was coming out of the bag. It seemed to never end. It was well more than they expected and most of them were already fantasizing about how they was going to spend it. Nick was relieved that the masked man had finally put his only son down. He had been dumping so much money in the gunman's hands that he seemed to forget about the gun he was holding.

Nick took in the room for the last time and could see that the men all had smiles under their mask as they closely watched the money being taken out of the bag. Nick knew this was his chance.

Chapter 10

The bag on Rena's back suddenly felt ten times heavier than it actually was. She imagined that the straps of the bag was digging into her skin, tearing her flesh apart. "Are you okay, young lady?" the sheriff asked, noticing Rena's physical condition.

"Ya . . . Yes Sir, I . . . I'm fine, just a little hot," she lied using her free hand to wipe the sweat off her face.

"So how do you like our little neighborhood?" Rena felt like the entire world had been lifted off of her shoulders. Here she was thinking the sheriff was about to bust her for drugs and he only wanted to make small talk. Relieved, she decided to engage the officer in a little conversation.

"I like it just fine."

"That's good, have you visited our exercise room yet?" The sheriff pointed in the opposite direction towards a lone building.

"Oh that's what's in that building. I always wondered."

The sheriff turned towards his cruiser then began walking away, stopped in mid-stride. "Well I have to go now, it was nice meeting you, Ms. . . ."

"Mrs. Rena Roberts," she said with a smile on her face thinking about the day when that title would actually become hers.

"Okay, Mrs. Roberts, you have a nice day." And with that he departed, driving his cruiser out of the parking lot and out of view.

Rena exhaled, the worse was finally over. She then looked towards her balcony and saw Rock was still there looking over at her. She looked at him and frowned, then made her way down the steps and up to the condo. Rock was waiting for her with open arms when she arrived. He grabbed the heavy bag from her, placing it on the floor.

Rock embraced her in a bone crushing bear hug. "Baby, I am so sorry. Had I known that was going to happen I would of never asked you to go out there."

"Are you all right?" Rock questioned as he released her and started checking her as if looking for bullet wounds. Rena's anger soon turned into joy, due to the fact that Rock paid so much attention, showing concern for her safety and wellbeing.

For the rest of the day Rock decided he would pamper her in an attempt to make up for sending her out there, and almost getting her busted with his drugs, money and guns.

Just as the sheriff was exiting the condo complex, Keith and Kevin were entering it. They saw Rena go in the building with a large duffle bag on her shoulders, wondering what was inside of it.

"What the hell Rena doing up so early? I thought she said she was so tired?" Kevin asked his brother.

"I don't know, but I wonder what she got in the bag." They pulled up, parking next to Rock's Porsche. They got out of the car and started walking up to the building.

"You know what, I bet that's work cousin Rock was talking about the other night."

"Yeah, but all that couldn't be work," Kevin responded.

"I don't know, but I definitely want to find out."

"Me too," Kevin said as he opened the door, only to see Rock embracing the woman he should have been hugging on.

Rock released Rena when the pair came in. "What's up little cousins?" Kevin did not respond. He just glared at Rena as he walked by and sat on the couch.

"What's up cousin," Keith said with a smile on his face, trying to make light of the situation.

"What's wrong with him?" Rock asked, referring to Kevin.

"He just having a bad day that's all. Don't worry about it," Keith said, eyeing the duffle bag on the floor. Rock put his arm around his little cousin and walked into the living room, then looked over his shoulder towards Rena. "Baby could you take that bag to your room for me?" Rena lugged the heavy bag to her room, put it in the closet, then rejoined the other sin the living room.

When she came in, Keith and Kevin were sitting on the couch while Rock was sitting opposite them on the lazy-boy. She decided to sit next to her man and straddled the arm of his chair. The entire scene looked like something straight out of a King of Egypt rerun. Rock was reclining on his throne with his queen by his side, dictating to his subjects.

"Listen," Rock said, looking over his cousins. "You guys ready to turn this shit up?" Kevin just shrugged his shoulders. "Well Kevin, do you want to get this money or not, because I'm not going to make this move with ya unless your heart is completely in it." Keith kicked his brother. "He with it cuz, just tell us what you want us to do."

"You sure you guys are ready?" Rock flared his arms up in the air. "Last call to get off the bus." He then looked at them sternly to emphasize his point. When no one spoke up, he took their silence as acquiescence.

"All right then, I'll be right back." Rock excused himself, walking to the bedroom. "BABY WHERE YOU PUT THAT BAG AT?"

"IN THE CLOSET," Rena responded.

Rock quickly bent into the closet, opened up the bag, then took all of his money out. He dumped his clothes over top the money, then returned with the bag and dumped it in the middle of the living room floor. Keith, Kevin and Rena sat there with their mouths wide open. They never seen that much coke and guns in their lives. Rock sat back down in the lazy-boy and gave them time to take in their new situation.

"Yo Keith, what coke go for up here?"

"Bout $1,500 a ounce."

"Okay, we gonna sell it for $1,300." He paused for a minute, then continued. "Let's see, that means we got 5 keys at 36 ounces per . . . that's $134,000 sitting there. There are three of y'all, so everybody gets $11,350 each."

Now it was time for Kevin to chime in. The prospect of him getting that much money at one time awakened him out of his hater-like trance.

"So let me get this straight, cuz. If we sell these 5 keys, you going to give us $11,000 a piece?"

"That's right, and since there is three of y'all, that means you only need to get rid of about a key and a half a piece."

"So what if we break it down?" Kevin asked with greed in his heart and larceny in his eyes.

"No, lil cousin, we got to do this my way. If we break this down it'll bring too much heat, because those $20 bags you thinking about selling, going to bring more customers and with more customers, comes more heat and we don't need that."

They nodded their heads in agreement. "Don't worry 'bout getting extra money out of this shift, more going come." Rock paused, then continued, "and for every 5 keys y'all sell for me. I'll give y'all the same $11.350 each."

Rock felt bad that he couldn't give them the usual rate of one key for every two sold. However, that was when he was able to break a key down into dimes. Now he was in the wholesale game, which was totally different. In the wholesale game a dealer gets paid a low percentage of the profits and makes up for it by selling his product faster to the street level hustlers, so he can flip his money more often.

"You guys have a digital scale?" Rock asked.

"Yeah, we use it to weigh our weed with," Rena replied with a smile.

"Okay baby, start bagging this shit up in ounces. I'll be right back, I need to go make a phone call." Rock went back to his room, dug through his clothes in the bottom of the closet, picked up his cellphone and dialed.

Placing the phone to his ear, "Come on Kya, pick up." Kya was sitting in his living room playing with his kids when his cellphone rang. He looked at the screen, didn't recognize the number, so he sent the call to voicemail and continued playing with his kids. Three minutes later his house phone rang. Kya was now starting to get a little paranoid. Here he was trying to bond with his children and someone he didn't even know was blowing up his phone.

He attempted to ignore it. However, after the phone wouldn't stop ringing, he had to go pick it up. "WHO A DAT, BUMBA CLOD, INTERRUPT ME TIME WIT ME PICKNEY?" Kya yelled with anger in his voice.

"Yo Kya what's good?" Kya couldn't believe his ears. His boy Rock finally got in touch with him and just in the nick of time. Ever since Rock went on the run, Kya had to tap into some of his old money.

"Good, good. My yout how you?"

"I'm hot to death striving to make something happen out here."

"Call me back Iree."

Rock hung up, then called him back on his cellphone. He and Kya had long since known, never to discuss business on a landline. They both invested in international cellphones, whose company did not use American satellites and cell towers.

"What's up my yout."

"Like I said before, I'm dumb hot right now."

"Okay, whatta ya need?"

"Nine door openers for one hundred. I'll give you the difference next time." Kya knew that Rock was asking him for nine kilo's for one hundred thousand dollars. He quickly did the math and estimated that Rock was asking him to take an eight thousand dollar short. However, he knew that he was good for it.

"Okay, me got dat for yew. Where you want it?"

"I want you to tow a junker up here with the work in it and I'll send it back with GWOP in it."

"Look, I have to go, but I'll text you the details. Iree, I'll holla my yout." And with that they hung up.

Kya relaxed for a moment in his easy leather chair with a happy countenance plastered on his ace. He was happy that his boy was alive and well, even happier that Rock called and ordered more product. Of course it was not the amount of product he expected to be selling Rock that month. However, he reasoned that once Reek came through with his part, it would be a substantial amount.

Kya couldn't wait to flip his eight million dollars with his Uncle Blocka back in Jamaica's Tivoli Gardens. When Kya inherited the family business, it had come with a large price to pay. Before his uncle died, he made him promise to flip his money only with Shota's from Tivoli Gardens, because they were the ones responsible for feeding many of the poor and disenfranchised people in Jamaica.

Kya felt good knowing that even though he made money from others' pain, at least he made a difference in the lives of his people back home. Kya wondered if Rock had known that his friend Reek was still alive and found it strange that he never asked about him. It finally dawned on him that maybe Rock didn't know that his boy Reek was still alive, when he left him last. After all, Reek was in pretty bad shape and barely hanging on to life. Paramedics had to resuscitate him quite a few times before he even made it to the hospital. Had it not been for Rock's tenant Luna calling the police, Reek might not be alive.

Rock went back into the living room and observed the trio bag up his cocaine ounce by ounce. He gently placed two hands on Rena's shoulders and stood over her, watching as she scooped up gram after gram of coke in a large metal spoon and placed it into a clear ziplock bag.

She paused only for a moment to look at Rock, then continued her business of bagging up. Rock looked at the cocaine in Rena's hands with some worry in his eyes. Most people wouldn't have noticed it, but to a seasoned vet like Rock, he knew that the cocaine wasn't mixed properly with the Bolivian cut he put on it. To the trained eye one could clearly notice this. He kicked himself in the ass for not taking the time out to properly mix the coke. However, he reasoned that since he was going to sell it wholesale as opposed to bottle for bottle, each ounce should at least be 65% pure.

"Okay y'all, I just got off the phone with my connect, so you could be rest assured that we going to see alot more shit than this." Rock paused for a second, then continued, "Normally I don't keep this much coke around me, so I'm going to spin off and hit up a motel, but don't trip while we out." Rock looked at Rena. "We going to find a stash spot for the shit that come in. Until then . . ." Rock moved over to the lazy-boy and sat down. "Y'all just move din here, so as long as y'all don't hustle out of the crib, you guys should be okay."

"How much y'all got left to bag up?"

"About half a key," Keith said with coke caked all over his bare hands.

"Okay, finish bagging up. You . . ." He pointed at Rena, "Come with me."

Rock grabbed the duffle back, put the guns back into it, then walked into the bedroom with Rena closely following behind him.

"Baby, we gotta get out of here." He put the bag on the floor. "Here, hold it open for me." Rena held the bag open and watched as Rock dumped bundle after bundle of money into it. She had never seen that much money in her life and was now starting to second guess whether or not she wanted to participate in Rock's new drug venture.

He paused for a moment and looked at the worry in Rena's eyes and decided to comfort her.

"Baby," he started, "I know this seems like alot to take on by yourself, and I could see that by the look on your face this is not for you."

"No baby, I want to help," Rena protested.

"And you will. How about you take care of the weed that y'all got left over and that way my cousin can concentrate on moving my work." Rena nodded her head in agreement.

Now you know that I'm going to give Keith and them your cut because now they have all 5 kilos." Rena looked a little hurt, however went along with it. "And if you're serious about us, then your cut is something you won't have to worry about."

"Are you serious?"

"No, the question is, are you serious?" Rena kissed and hugged Rock passionately. "Does that answer your question?"

"I guess it does."

"Here, hold onto this for me." Rock handed her a bundle of 50's wrapped up in a large rubber band. He then grabbed the bag and walked out of the room with Rena behind him.

"Listen y'all, a quick change of plans . . ."

"I knew this shit was coming," Kevin said under his breath.

"What was that?" Rock asked.

"Nothing," Keith replied. "What's up?"

"Like I was saying before." Rock looked at Kevin sternly. "Rena decided to knock that weed off y'all, instead of getting in the coke game."

He paused for a moment, letting his words sink in. "So y'all got to pick up on her part, which means y'all get $17,020 each now.

That news put a smile on their faces. "And if y'all get this shit right, I'll give y'all keys for 25."

"We got it cuz," they both said in unison with twin smiles planted firmly on their faces and with that Rock walked out the door.

Rena stood at the door and told Keith and Kevin she'd be back for the weed, then left after Rock. Once outside, Rock pulled out his keys, unlocking the Porsche, jumped in the passenger side, tossing the duffle bag onto the backseat.

Rena just stood there looking confused. It wasn't until Rock waved her in, that she had taken up possession in the driver's seat.

"You know how to drive dick, I mean stick?" Rock asked in a joking manner. Rena playfully pushed him, then started the car and pulled off.

"Where to?"

"First we need to find a decent hotel to check into." Rock turned on some 2Pac then reclined his seat. "Then we going to need storage for that new work."

At that moment Rena was relieved that she had decided to play only a small role in Rock's hustle. Just to confirm her wisdom, she asked him just how much coke he expected to get. "Oh, just 9 keys, which is going to be 12 after I'm finished working my magic on it," Rock said as if telling her about a vending machine business.

Rena turned onto the highway and smoothly entered traffic. "So, how much can you make off of that?"

Rock looked at her curiously, then he checked her, starting from her neck and continuing down to her breast. "What you wired or something?"

"Stop playing Boy," Rena said while playfully pushing him.

"Are you wired?" she asked, while checking Rock in his crotch area.

Rock laughed, then continued, "Nah, but seriously we should make close to half a million."

"A half a mission dollars?" Rena said, astonished on how nonchalantly Rock spoke about such a large amount of money.

"How much money do Keith and them get?" Rena asked with enthusiasm in her voice.

Rock was happy that his woman was so interested in his business and didn't mind teaching her all that he knew about the game.

"Well, technically they was supposed to make about 36 each, since we pushing weight, but I'm going to give them $50,000 since we should be good in Jamaica with all together over half a million dollars."

"You taking a big chance flipping your last."

"Yeah, but desperate times call for desperate measures. Besides, if they don't do their part, we won't have all the money for my connect." Rock paused, then added, "That's why I'm going to have you get $10,000 from them every time they make it."

Rena smiled, knowing that her new man put so much trust in her.

"Okay baby, we here. Park up, cop the room for a month, then meet me back at the car. We got some more business to take care of."

Chapter 11

The bullet struck the pillow next to Lanceen's head. Had she been just one inch to the left, she would have been dead. Lanceen wrestled the gun away from Cindy, then slapped her to the floor.

Cindy crashed to the side of the bed with a loud thud. Lanceen calmly strapped her gun back to her thigh holster, then jumped overtop of Cindy, then began to rain a barrage of punches onto the smaller woman's head, arms and stomach.

"YOU DUMB BITCH, YOU TRIED TO KILL ME!" Cindy folded herself into a ball and cried hysterically.

"I'm so sorry, I . . . I didn't mean it."

She continued to beat on her until she was tired. She collapsed on the floor next to her in a puddle of her own sweat.

Cindy went from crying hysterically to merely sniffling. "I'm sorry Miss Lanceen."

"SORRY IS NOT GOING TO FIX THIS SHIT," Lanceen said with anger in her voice.

"SHUT THE FUCK UP BITCH!" Cindy immediately stopped crying.

The realization that she was stuck in this bad situation had finally sunk in, and she decided at that very moment that if she was going to survive, she had better get with the program.

"What can I do to make it up to you?" she questioned, as she began to softly kiss Lanceen on her neck and lips.

"Nothing, bitch," Lanceen shouted, still angry about the attempt on her life. Cindy persisted on kissing and sucking on her erect nipples. Unable to remain mad, Lanceen relaxed and allowed Cindy to pleasure her. When Cindy began to trail down her body; kissing and caressing her, Lanceen immediately grabbed her gun and placed it under her head.

"Fool me twice, well you don't want to know what happens then," Lanceen thought out loud.

Though Cindy had been doing a good job at making up with her, Lanceen knew that from that moment on, she would never be able to trust Cindy again. This white bitch crazier than she anticipated and Lanceen made a mental note to always keep an eye on her.

Lanceen grabbed a handful of Cindy's hair and came in her mouth. Cindy unwillingly swallowed her essence, then went to the bathroom to tend her wounds. She turned on the light, then looked in the mirror. Cindy was startled at the sight of her horrible figure that was staring back at her.

The woman that stared back at her looked older. She had bags under her eyes, her cheeks were red and swollen and her head was black and blue. Surely the woman that stared back at her wasn't her.

She put her hands up to her face in amazement. *How could she have sustained so much extensive injuries in such a small amount of time*, she asked herself. Lanceen couldn't have been beating on her for the ten minutes and she looked like she had just stepped out of the ring with Mike Tyson.

Cindy began to weep, then stopped herself, reasoning that she had to be strong if she expected to make it through this. She grabbed a towel, wet it at one end and wiped her face clean with it.

When she emerged from the bathroom, Lanceen was sitting on the bed with the light on facing towards the bathroom.

"Bitch, sit down." When Cindy attempted to sit next to her, Lanceen forced her to sit in the seat she placed in front of her. When Cindy sat down she was eye-to-eye with the woman she attempted to murder just moments ago.

Lanceen just regarded her with a stern look for a minute. The awkward silence seemed to scare Cindy more than the fact that Lanceen had withdrawn her gun and was now silently staring at her with death in here eyes.

Suddenly she got up and lunged for her. Lanceen wrapped her hand around Cindy's small throat and squeezed as hard as she could. When Cindy opened her mouth in an attempt to breathe, Lanceen shoved the gun into it. She spoke in a law, barely audible tone. "Bitch, if you ever pull a gun on me again, I'm going to kill you and then I'm going to kill your kids."

The last part frightened Cindy the most. *Would this Federal Agent really kill her children*, she thought.

With tears in her eyes, she looked up at Lanceen and got her answer. Yes, this woman is crazy enough to go after her children.

She'd known from that moment on that she'd better play ball. "I'm sorry, Ms. . . . Ms. Lanceen. I promise I'll be good and do everything you tell me."

Lanceen withdrew her gun out of the young girl's mouth, then holstered it. She sat back down on the bed and regarded Cindy with a devilish smirk. "Do you know where Kevin and Keith live?"

"I know whe . . . where they used to. They moved about a month ago," Cindy managed to get out.

"So do you know where they live at this very moment?" Lanceen asked impatiently.

"Na. No, but I'm sure I can find out."

"You do that. I have a real surprise for them niggas."

"Who was on the phone with Keith?"

"That was Rena," Keith said as he counted out the $1,400 he'd just gotten for his first ounce sale.

"What that bitch want?"

"She told me that big cuz wants us to let her know after we make ten thou, so she could come pick it up." Kevin was furious.

"Why he want us to give it to her for? What, that nigga don't trust us?"

Kevin picked up his coat and began to walk out the door. "Let me get that key."

Keith tossed him a kilo. "What you going to do with it?"

Kevin stuffed the kilo inside his coat pocket. "I'm going to sell it. What the fuck you think I'm to do with it?"

"Please don't tell me you going down in Raleigh and fuck with that grimy ass dude Bre from Trenton."

"What's wrong with making a couple of dollars on the side?"

"What's wrong with it, is that Rock don't want us to sell it like that."

"What he don't know won't hurt him." And with that Kevin went out the door.

He jumped in the car and drove down to Raleigh to meet up with his new friend. When he got there, Bre was sitting in his usual spot selling crack on his front porch. He was not hard to spot. Bre had been the only one out there who was tall, brown-skinned with a big Muslim beard.

Bre was also very flashy with gold fronts on his bottom teeth, long platinum chains and a large platinum Movado watch.

Growing up in the rough part of North Trenton, Bre had always been a hot boy and when Kevin told him that he came into a couple of keys, Bre had immediately suggested that he let him break them down and make a bigger profit.

Kevin had been reluctant at first, however when Bre told him that he could get him a hundred grand a key, he was all in. What Bre had failed to mention to Kevin was the fact that he planned to split that hundred with him and that he also planned to put a twenty-five percent cut on the coke whenever he cooked it up.

Kevin jumped out of the car and greeted Bre with a handshake. Bre only 27 in age, was streetwise beyond his years and had known that it was best to have the product in his hand before he revealed his plan to split the money. "Let's go in the house." Kevin followed him into the house. "Have a seat. You want something to drink?"

"No thanks." Kevin was all business that evening and wanted to get this drop-off over with as fast as he could. He didn't like the fact that Bre sold drugs so openly.

"So, you think you could handle this much coke?"

"What, can Tiger Woods play golf? Of course I can handle a key."

Bre responded trying to instill confidence in him. "So did you bring it with you?"

Kevin pulled out the coke and handed it to him. "So when can I expect to get my money?"

"Soon my nigga. You see how much my crib popping. Feinds be in here all the time," Bree said over his shoulder, while walking into the kitchen.

"Well, call me when you make your first 5 stacks," Kevin said on his way out the door.

"Alright dog, I got you."

Bre was already at his stove preparing to cook up the coke he just picked up. He barely heard what Kevin just said. He was just happy to have seen him go.

Bre put a small amount of water into a pot, then brought it to a boil. He put a pair of latex gloves on, knowing he had to touch the coke and he didn't want any of the lethal substance to soak into his pores.

Once the water was hot enough, he placed the kilo into it and started whipping it with a large spoon. Had an innocent onlooker witnessed this sight, he would have thought that Bre was baking a cake the way he was vigorously pounding the large spoon into the coke batter.

He added water as needed until the cocaine became a thick paste. Then he added a box of his secret ingredient, baking soda. With a little more water and alot more mixing, Bre turned one kilo into a kilo and a quarter. To complete his task, he placed the entire mixture into the freezer, so it could dry and harden. He rubbed his hands together, anticipating the outcome of his chemistry.

Kevin jumped back into the car, feeling uneasy. It was something about Bre that he just couldn't trust. However, the prospect of his earning one hundred thousand dollars off of a key, was too good of an opportunity for him to pass up.

Besides, he reasoned, if anything was to go wrong, there was always plan B. Kill Bre and take his block.

Back at home, his brother Keith was worried sick about him. He should have been home by now, Keith said to himself, wearing a hole in the carpet, walking back and forth.

"He could have at least called me." Keith was not only worried about his twin brother, he was disgusted with him. Not only did he disobey Rock, he took the car with him, knowing that he had to make a drop off at 7:30 p.m. After his brother didn't show up, he was forced to meet the man on foot at the local supermarket.

Keith was no dummy, he made sure that he went to the supermarket first. This way, it gave him ample time to take four ounces he had and dump them in the garbage bin.

Since he wrapped the coke up in a brown paper bag, it looked just like the rest of the trash in the bin. When the man arrived, he insisted that he not exit the car. Instead he decided to lean into the driver side window and get the money and then he would call him and let him know where he could get his product.

The man reluctantly agreed and Keith walked a little way down the block and once he saw that the man wasn't looking, he hid in the bushes and counted the money. He then called the man and told him where the coke was and watched as he retrieved it.

Shortly after the man had pulled off, Keith made his way back to the condo, and to his surprise his brother was already there.

"What took you so long?" Keith sat the money down on the kitchen table.

"After I left Bre's house, I ran into some girl I haven't seen in awhile," Kevin said nonchalantly.

"So you mean to tell me that you had me walking to meet a custy so you could get some fucken butt?" Keith was furious. To him that was the last straw. Not only did he disobey their big cousin, he put him in danger by not being back on time.

"This wasn't any butt, this was my high school sweetheart Nicky that I haven't seen in a minute."

"I don't give a fuck if it was Nefertiti nigga, you should have been there." Keith slammed his coat to the floor, then sat down and started counting money.

Kevin realized that he hurt his brother. They usually did everything together and for the first time in life, he let his greed and jealousy cause him to abandon the most loyal person he had in his corner, his twin.

He put his hand over his brother's shoulder and spoke to him softly. "I'm sorry, you're right. I should have been there for you, ain't no butt worth your butt."

Keith looked up at his brother and they both broke out in laughter. Kevin sat down, then pulled out a wad of money from his back pocket. "Where you get that from?"

"From that two ounce sale I made yesterday."

"Let me see it so I can add it with this."

Kevin handed him the money and Keith counted it with the money he had and it was about $200 short of 10 stacks. "I'm gonna call Rena up anyway and tell her to come get this." Kevin balled his face up. He still wasn't happy that he had to turn over his money to disloyal ass Rena. Besides, he questioned what was wrong with Rock picking up his **own** damn money? When Keith called Rena and told her what they had, she was over there within the hour to pick up the money.

When she arrived in Rock's black Porsche 911, Kevin was overwhelmed with jealousy. As soon as she came to the door, Kevin was there to greet her. He shoved the bag of money up into her stomach. The force caused her to take a few steps back just to maintain her balance. She walked out without saying a word, clutching the bag of money as if it was a security blanket.

Once she was safely back in the car, the waterworks began. She didn't want to give him the satisfaction of seeing her cry. She didn't want him to know that he affected her like that. Sure the blow to the stomach, when he handed her the money was painful, however it wasn't the physical pain that had caused her to cry, It was the fact that she had always considered Kevin to be her brother and he had never treated her in such a way.

Meanwhile, Rock was pacing the hotel room worried about Rena. This had been her first pick up and he was trusting her with alot of responsibility. He would prefer to pick up his own money, however he was currently a fugitive from justice.

Rock then went from worry to pure impatience. In the time that Rena had left, his aunt Puddin called and informed him that his car was there. Without Rena, he had no way of making it over there and no way of paying the connect all of the money. He needed Rena's part in order to pay the full amount.

When Rena arrived an hour late, Rock had been furious. "Where the fuck you been?"

Rena just dropped the bag of money on the hotel room floor and started crying. Rock went from furious to confused. He had no idea that his words would effect her that badly. He felt terrible that he even yelled at her. With guilt and regret in his heart, he hugged her passionately. "I'm sorry baby," he whispered into her ear. "It was just that I was so worried about you." He continued. "I know I gave you a big responsibility, with all the stuff you've been through. Maybe I should have come up with a better plan, like getting the money myself."

Rena stopped crying instantly then looked him dead in his eyes. "Baby I can't let you do that, you're on the run and I don't know what I would do if you ever got locked up." Rock began to protest but was cut off by Rena.

"I wasn't crying about the pick up or what you said. I was crying because one of my best friends just died," Rena lied. Basically, Kevin did not actually die, however he died mentally and spiritually as her friend.

Rock attempted to hug her again. This time Rena pushed him away, wiped away her tears and handed him the bag. "I'll be fine baby, right now we have some business to handle."

That's what Rock loved about Rena, how fast she recovered from injury and how strong and determined she was. These are the types of qualities Rock felt made the perfect woman. Once inside the car Rock decided to engage Rena in small talk. "So how's your weed business going?"

"Great baby. At first I didn't know if I could handle the whole load, but I had some unexpected help from my white girlfriend Cindy."

"White girl?" Rock repeated with a mock look of confusion on his face. "I never knew you missed white girls like that."

"Yeah. I met Cindy a couple of years ago, when I was in my wild club days." She made a left and jumped onto the highway.

"So, you say you sold her all that weed?"

"Just about, in fact she asked if I had some powder too."

Chapter 12

The last item that Nick pulled out of the bag was a gun. The robbers were so transfixed on all the money that they hardly even noticed the gun he was holding in his hand. Nick shot the first intruder and all hell broke loose.

Nick hit the closest robber with three quick shots to the stomach. The slugs from the .32 revolver ripped through him and immediately aired him out. Before the intruder had really known what hit him, he was on the floor clutching his stomach, fighting for air.

The shots seemed to have awakened the other three accomplices. They started wildly firing into the apartment. Reek sprung into action, shooting and wounding the two gunman nearest to him, however, not before the two men were able to get off a couple shots themselves.

One stray bullet had caught Nick high in the back of his neck as he lunged to shield his newborn son from the gunfire with his own body. Nick lay dead on top of his son.

During the melee, Tiesha had stood up. Her motherly instincts taking over and attempted to run over to protect her baby, but had gotten cut down by the last of the gunmen's bullets. At that point the gunman was hysterical and was not willing to take any more chances, so he shot at anything that was moving.

Before he had the opportunity to fully turn in Reek's direction and take him out, he was shot in the side of the head by Peewee. *I should have checked that lil nigga for guns*, the man thought before passing out dead on the floor, right near the money he paid his life for attempting to steal.

"Quick Peewee, get the money." Peewee got up slowly and began putting the now bloody money back into the bag. His head hurt from the pistol whipping and he was still very drowsy. Reek took in the room, then looked down at Nick. Tough he hadn't known him very well, he still felt bad for him. The man had been a brave and loyal soldier. Peewee had finally collected all of the money.

As they walked out the door, Peewee could hear the muffled sounds of a baby crying underneath big Nick. He stopped in his tracks. "I hear something."

"We don't have no time to deal with that shit now Peewee. Let's break," said Reek.

"We just can't leave that baby like this." Peewee handed Reek the bag of money, then attempted to unsuccessfully pull the limp body out of Big Nick off of the suffocating child.

Reek, unable to leave his little man, reluctantly helped Peewee lift the limp body of Big Nick off of his dying baby. Though the baby was dark brown in complexion, his face turned blue due to a lack of air. Once the baby was able to breathe again, he let it be known by crying in the loudest tone his small lungs could carry.

Peewee headed out the door, clutching the baby tightly to his chest, while Reek paused over the bodies of the wounded men and put them out of their misery. By the time Reek exited the building, it seemed like the whole neighborhood had awakened because there was a crowd of men, women and children on both sides of the building.

The scene reminded Reek of the Soul Train line and he was the main dancer stuck in the middle. As soon as he left the building, all eyes was on him. Reek lifted his gun in the air and fired until his clip was empty. The crowd instinctively ran for cover, no one wanting to make the cover of tomorrow morning's Star-Ledger newspaper.

Reek descended the steps of the building content in the fact that his little exploits had worked in dispersing the crowd. To his surprise, Peewee had already had himself and baby Tariq strapped in the truck and ready to go.

He jumped in the truck and pulled off wildly with no specific destination in mind. He picked up his phone and dialed the numbers to Kya's phone. After a few rings, Kya answered. "Hello, where you at?"

"Me at home, what up."

"I got a little situation and I need to come holla at you."

"Good, me was just about to call yew. When yew get in come in the backyard airy."

"True, I'll be there in a minute."

Reek hung up the phone feeling confused. he had no idea why Kya wanted him to come into the backyard when he had got there. "Did you see all of them people out there?"

"Yeah Peewee. Them niggas was making it hot out there. We might have to lay low for a minute."

"Where we going to go?" Peewee asked, while attending to baby Tariq. The baby had finally settled down a little bit and Peewee was just making sure that he was alright.

"We going to my connect house right now. I just need time to figure out our next move." Peewee felt closer than ever to his O.G. Reek. He loved the fact that he had included him in his plans to lay low.

When they arrived at Kya's house, he was waiting for them in the backyard. "Who picknay dat?" Kya asked, referring to the baby that Peewee held in his arms. Reek explained the situation about what had happened at Big Nick's house. "Dat okay. Maybe dis surprise me give yew help dat," Kya said as he motioned them to follow him.

They went down a narrow path filled with high weeds and bushes until they came across what appeared to be an abandoned barn. The broken down barn looked so awkward in a neighborhood filled with million dollar homes.

I guess that's why this place is so far away from all the houses, Reek thought.

"Come," Kya said while standing at the barn's entrance with the door opened and a devilish grin plastered firmly on his dark face. The sun had begun to descent behind the horizon, which caused the clouds and sky to become emblazoned with a strong red color. Usually Reek would have considered this a beautiful sight, but for some reason that night sky, coupled with the queasy feeling he had, almost looked satanic.

He could see a dim light flickering on the straw littered barn floor. As they got closer, he could hear faint grunts and moans coming from the inside. They all went into the barn. Peewee clutched the baby in horror at what he saw inside the barn. There was two fat white men without a stitch of clothing on, awkwardly bent over a large wooden pole. They were beaten and sweating profusely. Their feet and hands were bound together, involuntarily causing their bodies to be overstretched in a bending position.

Reek imagined that the wooden pole that they were bent over was uncomfortably digging into their large white bellies. However, the gags that they had taped to their mouths prevents them from protesting. Kya walked over in front of the two men, grabbed them roughly by their hair, then violently jerked their heads up. "Reek, come here. Yew recognize dem?"

Reek came around and looked at the men attentively. "They look kinda familiar, but I don't know them."

"Well, dis D Bobby lion scum who do yew dirty."

Reek jumped into action and immediately started wailing on the two men.

Kya just sat there and watched. After, Reek looked like he would kill the men if he allowed him to continue. Kya finally stopped him. Kya then waved his hand.

"Come." From behind, two men in a remote section of the barn stepped out and Monay walking with two large donkeys. Monay gently stroked the big donkey's dicks simultaneously until she felt them stiffen under her touch. The donkeys began to sweat and pant wildly. Their eyes grew wide with excitement.

"Yo Kya, what type of freak shit you invite me up here to see?" Reek asked with confusion in his eyes.

"Watch and see my yout."

Reek watched as Monay led the animals to the rear of the men. Once she had the donkeys positioned over the top of the men, she again began to stroke the donkey's penis, rubbing them up and down the cracks of the men's asses, prompting them to do their worst. Within seconds, the donkeys were mounting them, stroking them with 20 inches of dick, hard enough to cut diamonds with. The donkeys showed the two men no mercy. At first they seemed to run into problems with the lack of lubrication. However, after a couple of strong strokes, the blood from the men's rectums fixed that problem. Peewee took that moment to exit the barn. Surely that was no place for an infant baby.

Reek cringed at the sight of the two white men being violated by the donkeys. However, he felt no remorse for them. You do dirt and you get dirt, that was his motto. They all sat there and just watched as the animals literally fucked the two white officers to death. "What we going to do with them now?" Reek asked, knowing the potential repercussions behind killing not one, but two white officers of the law.

"Don't worry, my yout." Kya placed a comforting hand on his shoulder. "Me a feed dem to me gators." Kya laughed hysterically as they walked out of the barn.

Reek noticed that before leaving, the old strange woman whispered something into Kya's ear that caused his facial expression to contort into horror, then confusion and back to a blank stare.

He wanted to ask Kya about the old woman and what she had whispered into his ear, however he didn't want to pry.

The next morning Reek woke up early and had creeped back down to the barn. He wanted to know what had become of the two white officers. When he opened the barn door, he was surprised to see that the barn had been completely emptied. Reek went over to the spot where the men were mutilated and suddenly relived the whole scene. There he was again standing there next to Kya, pretending to enjoy the horrific event of two men being raped by farm animals.

Though Reek hated what the men had done to him and wanted revenge, he never imagined or wanted the men to die in such a way. No man should die like that. Reek could still hear their shrill moans. He shook his head in disbelief, trying to shake off the horrifying sounds coming out of his head. However, for some reason they would not leave.

Maybe I need some fresh air, he thought to himself as he stumbled out of the barn. When the screams persisted, he realized that they weren't actually coming from his head, but from the mansion. In the distance Reek could see his little man Peewee running around in circles, looking through bushes and underneath cars as if he just lost his best friend.

He called to him to try to find out if he was okay. However, Peewee didn't respond. Instead, he just continued to scream and look around frantically. "What the fuck is wrong with him?" Reek mumbled, as he stalked over to his comrade. He grabbed Peewee by his shirt and began to shake him.

After, Peewee seemed to calm down. He wiped the tears from his eyes, then Reek released him. *Maybe this too much for my little man*, he thought to himself. *The shit he's done and seen in the last 24 hours must be getting to him.*

He sat him down on the mansion steps. He could tell that Peewee was still visibly shaken. "What's wrong my little man?"

"I went to sleep last night with the baby in my arms and when I woke up he was gone," Peewee said, starting to become emotional again.

"Come on Peewee, let's go back inside the house and holla at my man. I'm sure he could shed some light on this. I bet you the baby with the maid right now getting fed. You worrying for nothing," Reek assured him.

They stepped inside and found Kya sitting in his favorite chair, enjoying his morning blunt. He greeted them with a smile and offered them some of the weed. "No thanks Kya, but there is something you could help me with," Reek said.

"What dat?" Kya answered casually.

"It seems my man lost the baby he had."

"Oh dat. My people Monay take dee Pinkney home wit she."

Peewee and Reek couldn't believe what they just heard.

"Me know," Kya continued. "Yew wanted to keep dee Pinkney, but Monay suggest she take him. Dee fugitive life, no life for he."

Although Reek didn't like it, he had to admit that Kya was right. However, Peewee didn't take to the news as well and began to spaz out. Reek grabbed a hold of him and walked him up the stairs before he could go completely haywire.

"Listen Peewee, I know you liked that kid, but to keep it real, we both know we couldn't take him with us."

"Why not, I could've taken care of him. You wouldn't have to worry about him." Peewee sat down on the bed, still shaken up.

"We both know we couldn't be laying low with no missing baby associated with no bodies." He looked him in the eyes. "What would it look like if 80-8 caught us with that baby?"

"To be honest with you, I'm kinda glad Monay or whatever her name is took that baby." Reek knew his words were harsh, but he had to say them and Peewee needed to hear them.

"Do you honestly think dat baby better off with crazy old lady than with us?"

"Yeah. First of all, she is an old woman. She knows what to do with a baby." Reek lied. In fact, he thought the baby probably would have been better off left in the middle of the wood bridge mall than with that crazy ass bitch Monay, but he couldn't tell his little man that. It would of only made matters worse.

He decided wisely to change the subject. "Peewee, I was thinking last night that the best thing for us to do was to holla at my boy Rock."

"Rock, ain't that the coward ass nigga left you for dead at his house?"

"Watch your mouth Peewee. If it wasn't for him, I wouldn't be where I'm at now," Reek disciplined. "Listen to me. Rock is one of the bravest, most loyal niggas I know. I'm sure if he thought he could've saved me that night, he would have."

"So why didn't he?"

That was the one question Reek was unable to answer, but something he surely intended to find out. He ran down the steps and found Kya still sitting in the same spot.

"What's wrong my yout, yew friend alright?" Kya asked with little concern on his face.

"He cool Kya, but I have a question for you."

Reek sat on the couch across from him and regarded him seriously. "Do you know where Rock at?"

"Oh me forget to tell yaw. Rock in Nort Carolina."

"When was the last time you talked to him?"

Dem boys just ordered 9 from me, perfect Reek thought to himself. "He still moving work, maybe we could connect and make it happen. That is, as soon as I find out why he left me dying on his living room floor.

"Listen Kya, I'm in a big jam since me and Rock hot. I'm going to check him out down there."

"IREE," Kya responded, waiting impatiently to see where Reek was going with this.

"I'm sure he got coke on smash up there already. Soon I'm going to need some diesel." That got Kya's attention.

He had just run into a Dominican connect from Patterson who had some good prices on dope, but had turned him down because he didn't have the clientele for it. He could now get with the Dominican connect and charge Reek a couple of extra points for whatever he wanted. "What chew need?"

"Alot, depending on the number." Kya did the math quickly in his head. The Dominican guy said that he would give him dope at 39 dollars a gram, so if he charged Reek 45 a key, he could make 6 thousand off of each key.

"I give yew for 45."

"Okay, cool. I need two of them, but I only got 69. Listen Kya, I need to dump my truck. I'll trade you it for your Chrysler and the difference." *Rock had taught him very well in the art of negotiation,* Reek thought to himself. He knew that Kya couldn't resist that deal.

Even though his Cadillac truck was hot from the shooting, it was still worth at least 60 thousand dollars on the street. Kya quickly agreed, did the paperwork on the cars, met his connect and completed the deal with Reek, al in one day. By the time Reek and Peewee had hit the road, he only had two kilos of heroin and a thousand dollars to his name.

That's where him and Rock differed. Rock was the kind to save money while Reek lived more of a lavish life. So while Rock was prepared for a quick getaway, he wasn't. Reek felt very uncomfortable in the small car. He couldn't remember the last time he owned such a cheap automobile. Kya had felt terrible that he had stolen little Tariq from the sleeping Peewee and gave him to crazy ass Monay. He couldn't fathom why she wanted a baby as payment for two murders. However, he had his theories.

Chapter 13

After picking up the drugs and putting the money into its place, Rock and Rena drove to their storage unit and put the work in a metal safe on the back of the unit, then covered it with a dirty old quilt. Two weeks later Keith and Kevin had finally finished off the work that Rock had given them. With all of the payouts, the thirty-four thousand to Keith and Kevin, along with eight grand that he owed to Kya, Rock had made roughly ninety-two thousand dollars. Rock and Rena went down to the bank, and he took out a safety deposit box in her name and put ninety thousand into it. The other two he put into his pocket.

Meanwhile, Kevin was pacing the floor of the condo wearing a hole in the rug. He had his hand gripped tightly to his 9-millimeter, waving it awkwardly, side to side while he talked to himself. "That nigga Bree think he slick. He said I was going to make a hundred thousand off that key." All Keith could do was sit on the couch and helplessly watch as his brother angrily worked through his problem. When Kevin returned to Bree's house to collect his money, Bree had given him some bullshit run-around about how he had to take shorts because the coke wasn't good and how some of his runners got caught and he had to use part of the money for bail. At the end of the conversation Bree had put his head down and handed him a measly fifty-thousand dollars. Kevin was furious and thought about killing him right there on the street. However, when Bree told him that he'd known some dudes that were interested in buying two keys from him for a hundred grand, he changed his mind.

What Kevin didn't know was that the keys were actually for Bree, and he was using his money to buy them. After Bree had cooked the key up that Kevin gave him, it had come out to be a key and a quarter, so all Bree had to do was sale it at one hundred dollars a gram and he had made one-hundred and twenty-five thousand dollars. He gave Kevin fifty of that and added the last twenty-five thousand from his stash to the rest, which gave him a total of one hundred grand for his next flip. Kevin was upset that he only made an extra thirty-two thousand dollars on the whole deal, and in anticipation of getting the full amount he went on a spending spree, buying everything from diamond rings to watches and gold chains. The shopping spree caused him to spend all his profits, so when it was time to pay Rock, he had just enough left to cover the debt.

Keith was even more upset because he needed to add Kevin's half of the money with his own in order to take advantage of Rock's offer to sell them kilos at twenty-five thousand a piece.

Rena had informed them that the new shipment was in, and it was fire. And he expected to be able to purchase his first key at this juncture.

"I'm going to call big cuz and see if he'll let us get one for seventeen."

"But cuz said he going give it to us at twenty-five, and that's the cheapest I ever heard," Kevin said skeptically, then continued, "What make you think he going do something like that for us and we short?"

"Well, it's worth a try. The worst thing he could do is say no," Keith said finally getting Rock on the phone.

"Yeah, what up?"

"This Keith."

"Oh, what's up lil cuz?" Rock said.

"Listen, we went to grab one of those things off you, but we a lil short."

"How short?" Rock interrupted.

"Eight thousand short," Keith said while putting his head down.

"YOU MEAN TO TELL ME THAT OUT OF THIRTY-SIX THOUSAND DOLLARS, SEVENTEEN IS ALL Y'ALL GOT LEFT?" Rock couldn't believe what he was haring. He started questioning whether or not his little cousin was capable of handling the coke business.

"But, but big cuz."

Rock interrupted him again. "BIG CUZ MY ASS!" A pause, then he continued, "ONE OF THE REASONS I OFFERED Y'ALL TWENTY-FIVE A KEY IN THE FIRST PLACE WAS FOR Y'ALL TO COME INTO Y'ALL OWN!"

"I know, but—"

Rock calmed down and said, "Don't worry about it, I'll take the difference out y'all cut of the weed that Rena sold."

Keith had been so busy running around selling coke that he had totally forgotten all about their cut form the weed money.

"I'll have Rena come pick that gwop up and drop that off to y'all."

"Okay, big cuz, and good looking on that."

"Ain't nothing lil cuz, y'all family," Rock said, then continued, "I'm going also have her drop off a lil somen somen extra for y'all." And with that they both hung up.

After Rena dropped her man off at the hotel, she received an order form Keith for one key, so back out the door she went.

She drove all the way back across town to the storage unit, retrieved the kilo, then had to drive all the way back to Keith and Kevin's condo.

Once she arrived, she parked in a secluded part of the parking lot, then called the condo, hoping that Keith was the one that picked up.

Her prayers was answered.

"Hello!"

"What's up Keith. I'm downstairs right now."

"Well, come on up."

"Sorry Keith I can't do that." Rena put her head down.

"Why not?" Keith said, though he had a good idea why she didn't want to come upstairs.

"Is Kevin there?" she asked with a hint of fright in her voice.

"Yeah, he up here wearing a hole in our rug."

"Well, you know he not feeling me right now. Ever since I started messing with y'all cuzzen he been acting up."

"He just going through a transitional faze. He'll come around; you know how he feels about you."

"Yeah, I know," Rena sighed. "But that's no excuse for the way he been treating me lately."

"Just give him some time. He just got to get used to the idea of you and my cuzzen being together."

"Well, I still have a little more running around to do before I head in, sooo if you don't mind can we make this happen?"

"DAMN GIRL YOU MUST BE SPENDING TOO MUCH TIME WITH MY CUZZEN. YOU EVEN STARTING TO SOUND LIKE THAT NIGGA."

With that they both laughed, because they knew what Keith was saying was true.

Five minutes later Keith was peering through the drive's side of the porch. "So, what you got for me?"

"What you got for me?" Rena countered, with a mock hardcore drug dealer look on her face.

Keith rested one arm on the roof of the car, and with the other reached into his back pocket and retrieved a brown envelope. He handed it to her with a smirk on his face.

"What you smirking at?"

"You, lady cocaine. You really starting to look like a real live drug dealer."

"Whatever," Rena said as she quickly counted the money, and watched her surroundings all at the same time. Rena then popped the trunk and instructed Keith to grab the black duffle bag.

Soon after returning he paused for a minute to talk to her. "Damn girl, what you got in this bag, a missile launcher?"

Rena started the car's engine, indicating that their conversation and business transaction was concluded. However, Keith pressed on, "So what is it?"

"You'll seeee," she teased, smiling as she pulled off.

Keith walked back to the condo with a cocky stride, content that everything had worked out and he was able to cop his first kilo, in spite of a lack of cooperation on the part of his twin brother.

Of course he understood that his brother did make an effort, but they was going to need more than just an effort if they was going to survive in the coke business.

Since the kilo was purchased with mostly his money, he thought of giving his brother only six ounces of it. Besides, that was more than fair considering the small amount of money he contributed to it. However, he decided against it, opting to split the key with his brother, but this time it was going to be his way.

Keith had found logic in the way Rock told him to hustle and had decided to stick with selling his coke ounce for ounce or key for key, whichever one came first.

Meanwhile, Bree was starting to get agitated at how slow Kevin was. He supposed to been over his house with that kilo hours ago. It was bad enough that when he called and ordered two, this nigga claimed he only had one at the time. And on top of all that, he had two sexy ass female customers waiting to buy one of them right now.

Though Bree never knew the black woman nor the white one that was now sitting in his home, they both seemed cool. And since they offered to buy his kilo for fifty thousand, he figured he could make a quick buck of them. However, he was afraid that if Kevin didn't get there soon the two females would walk, and he would be out of a ten-thousand-dollar profit.

"Why don't you calm down, relax and have a seat. We not going nowhere big boy," Lanceen said while winking at Cindy.

Cindy just smiled awkwardly. Lanceen elbowed her roughly when Bree had turned his back.

"I can't understand what' staking this nigga so long." He sat down, then jumped right back up. "I called him over an hour ago."

"Just calm down baby and relax. Like I said before we not going nowhere." She picked Cindy on the lips, then looked at him seductively.

That got Bree's attention, because he stopped in his tracks, then sat down across from them, licking his lips and staring.

Suddenly, Kevin steps through the door, breathing heavily as if he had run there. He caught his breath, surveyed the room, then said, "Ah Ms. L longtime no hear."

"I been kinda busy getting rid of that weed you gave me," Lanceen said with a smile.

"And damn Cindy, I see you in everything but a casket."

"Don't sound like a bad idea," Cindy mumbled, then flinched in anticipation of getting punched by Lanceen. When none came, she relaxed a little.

Bree stood up and wrapped his arms around Kevin's shoulders. Kevin shrugged his hands off of him. "Let's just get this straight, we are not homies. The only reason I came over here is to handle business. So what's good?"

Lanceen could see the tension developing between the two men and decided to step in before it escalated. "Come on Kevin, let's go out to your car and talk business." She grabbed him by the hand and led him outside. When Bree tried to protest, she assured him that he would still receive his just due.

"So, you the big man here?" Lanceen said while wrapping her arms around his waist.

"Well, I wouldn't say all that, but I am pretty big," he replied with a sexual pun in his voice.

"I bet you are," she said while licking her lips seductively.

Once they got into the car she tore into Kevin's pants, then began to swallow his hammer. The sudden sexual act was so unexpected that Kevin was done in sixty seconds.

If he had any thoughts of this girl not liking him, those fears was now and forever put to rest. Lanceen wiped her mouth off, pulled out a hand mirror from her purse, then began to reapply her lip gloss. Kevin took this opportunity to give her the once over. She still dressed sexy and fly. However, he did notice that she had gotten fatter than when he first met her.

"So, now that we got that out of the way, let's talk numbers," Lanceen said, not missing a beat.

"Okay, what you got?"

"You show me yours; I'll show you mines," she countered.

"Well, you've already seen what I'm working with," Kevin said, referring to his penis. "Working with a monsta, working with a monsta."

Lanceen inwardly laughed at him, thinking to herself if he only knew how insignificant his penis was in comparison to his big cousin's. However, she'd decided some time ago that if she was going to get Rock, she was going to have to take a couple hits. And if she had to suck every little dick nigga in this town to get to her prize, then she would. Her mouth was open season, she reasoned. However, her butt and pussy belonged to one man.

"Ohh daddy, you felt sooo biggg in my mouth that I thought your cock was going break my little jaw," Lanceen's seductive words put Kevin's little soldier back on attention. She noticed and decided to give him one more pleasurable explosion before getting down to real business.

She again unbuttoned his jeans, gently removed his cock, bent over, and put it in her mouth. Lanceen's mouth was warm and wet. She teased him with her tongue, swirling it around the head of his dick, then deep throating him. Every time her head went down, her wet mouth made a sucking sound.

Kevin was determined to last longer than before. However, to his surprise, Lanceen sucked his dick like a seasoned pro, and he came faster than before. When he bussed, he grabbed a handful of her hair and thrust his hips upward to meet with her lips.

When she was finished, Lanceen went right back into business mode. "So how much?"

"Nine inches."

She playfully slapped him on his shoulder, then laughed, "No, I mean for the key."

"Oh, for you forty-six-eight."

"That's what's up. Your man Bree was trying charge me fifty-five."

Kevin's face turned grim. "FIRST AND FOREMOST THAT NIGGA NOT MY MAN. SECONDLY . . ."

"Hold on, hold on. Wait baby, I didn't mean to spoil the mood. I thought y'all was cool." She put a calming hand on his shoulder.

After Kevin finally calmed down, they completed their transaction. Before departing, Lanceen made sure to arrange a proper date with him when he found some time.

Kevin pulled off thinking about the bomb head he was just blessed with, and the big score him and his brother just made.

Meanwhile, Lanceen walked back into Bree's house after depositing the kilo underneath the passenger seat of her car.

"Cindy, go wait in the car for me. I'll be right out."

"We . . . we . . . still going see my?"

"YEAH BITCH, I'M GOING TAKE YOU TO SEE YOUR DAMN KIDS. NOW GO WAIT FOR ME IN THE CAR!" Lanceen yelled.

Cindy just put her head down and did as she was told. It had been weeks since she pulled a gun out on her and lately Lanceen's been pretty nice to her. Cindy was even able to convince her to let her see her kids, and she didn't want to do anything to fuck that up.

Lanceen wasn't too bad, Cindy reasoned. In fact, she was starting to get used to the idea of being with another woman. She had no idea that waking up every morning to an intense orgasm from another woman's mouth could be so pleasurable, and how quickly she would get turned out.

Lanceen closed the door behind her, then locked it. "I don't have any more money left big boy, but maybe we could work out some other type of arrangement."

Bree looked at her like she was stupid. The nerve of her offering him sex in place of ten thousand dollars. He looked at her stomach, and could clearly see that she was pregnant, and *probably by that nigga Kevin*, he thought to himself.

"Oh, I see you noticed that I'm carrying," Lanceen lifted up her shirt a little bit too far, purposely revealing her erect nipples with her baby bump. "This lil nigga in my stomach won't mine if mommy get a lil somen somen."

Bree never said a word, h just stared at her with lust in his eyes. The truth was he did want to fuck her ever since she showed up on his block asking for coke. The fact that she was pregnant didn't bother him a bit. In fact, he loved fucking pregnant girls, because they pussy was wetter and tighter than other girls. Besides, hew as contemplating on robbing her anyway. In his book getting some pregnant pussy on top was a plus.

"I seen the way you been looking at me. Don't tell me you don't want none of this tight pussy," she said as she kissed him on the neck, then reached into his pants and massaged his penis to stiff erection.

Bree began to undo Lanceen's jeans before she stopped him. "Hold on big daddy, no condom, no climb in."

"I'll be right back," he said as he rushed back to his room to retrieve his condom and gun. For some reason it was something about her he just didn't trust.

While Bree was bending over to get his gun, he felt the cold steel press against the back of his head. "Now what was you planning on doing with that big boy?" Lanceen asked looking at the nine-millimeter he held in his hands.

"I hope that's not what I think it is?" Lanceen asked, griding her .40 cal deeper into his head.

Bree mentally kicked himself in the ass for letting a pregnant girl get the drop on him. He secretly hoped that this story never got out.

"If you thinking this a fully loaded .40 cal hand cannon pointed to the back of your dome, then you're right. Now, put that rachet back in the drawer and close it up before you hurt yourself."

Bree did as she instructed, then Lanceen smacked him hard on the head with the butt of her gun.

"So, what was you planning on doing with that?"

Before he could answer, Lanceen smacked him on the head with the gun again, only this time twice as hard. The blow almost caused him to lose consciousness.

I gotta think of something quick. I can't take too many more hits like this from this broad, he thought to himself. "Th . . . the money underneath my mattress shorty, ple . . . please don't hit me in my head like that no more," Bree managed to say in spite of himself.

You would find in life that even the hardest of gangsters, when threatened with the fear of death, would say or do anything to get out of a mortal situation. And to Bree this was the closest he'd ever come to death.

Laying on his bedroom floor, barely hanging on to consciousness, he vowed to himself that if Allah allowed him to make it through this, he would turn over a new leaf and get back on his deen. Just as soon as he wrapped his hands around this bitch's throat and choked the living life out of her.

"I DON'T WANT YOUR FUCKIN' MONEY," was the last thing Bree heard before everything went black.

"Now, that's how you do business," Lanceen mumbled proudly to herself as she handcuffed Bree, then freely rumbled through his house stuffing money and drugs into her pants and purse.

Chapter 14

Rena returned to the hotel looking exhausted. Rock sat up in the bed and was about to get up to greet her. "No baby not right now, I'm beat. I'm sweaty and I need a shower."

Rock laid back down as Rena tossed him a bag full of money, took off her shirt and went into the bathroom. He started counting money while listening to Rena turn the shower on.

He put a big smile on his face content that his plans was starting to come together. At this rate he'd be out of the county and retired from the game in no time.

Sure his cousins was fucking up a little bit, however, he planned on fronting them some work and matching whatever they came to buy the next time. *That should put you on your feet*, Rock thought to himself. The sound of his cellphone ringing on the nightstand damn near gave him a heart attack.

The room had been so quiet that the loud cellphone sounded like an alarm system. Rock grabbed his heart, then reached over to retrieve the phone.

"Yo, what's up?"

"What's up Rock?" This time Rock almost really had a heart attack.

Was his mind playing tricks on him or was he really communicating with the dead? "Ra . . . Reek?"

"Yeah, it's me my nigga. What's good?"

"Reek, how is you doing this?"

"Rock, you tripping. What you mean how I'm doing this. Kya gave me your math."

"Kya dead too?"

"No Rock, ain't nobody dead. In fact, I'm about to cross into South Carolina right about . . ." A pause, then "NOW!"

"I'll believe it when I see it. Until then I'll text you my math," Rock said.

"Alright, well be there, one love." And wit that they both hung up.

Rock immediately jumped to his feet and put his blue shirt and black shirt and black Polo jeans on. He then went to the dresser and put his Smith and Wesson 500 in the small of his back.

It wasn't that he didn't trust Reek or anything. It was just a habit, like putting your socks on before your boots. Guns was just part of the hustler's uniform.

"Baby, I'm going to step out for a minute, okay?"

"Huh?"

"I SAID I'M GOING TO STEP OUT FOR A MINUTE. I GOT SOME BUSINESS TO HANDLE," Rock yelled.

"OKAY, I LOVE YOU TOO BABY!"

Rock stepped out onto the sidewalk and lit up a fresh Newport.

He thought about leaving her a small note explaining where he was going, since she obviously didn't hear him over the shower. However, reasoned that he should be returning soon he decided against it.

Damn my boy Reek still alive. An overwhelming sense of joy took over his heart, as he dragged lazily on the cigarette.

Meanwhile, Reek drove by Rock three times before he stopped in the middle of the parking lot. He had been so busy looking for the room number that he just now noticed Rock.

The Chrysler 300M didn't go unnoticed by Rock either. He didn't know what was going on with this strange car, but since it drove by him three times, then parked right in front of him, it was starting to make him kinda nervous. So he did what any other fugitive from justice would do in his situation. He reached around his back and put his hand on his gun.

The tinted window of the passenger side slowly rolled down halfway. Rock peered in from a safe distance and didn't recognize the young brown skinned male figure inside.

"YO, WHO DAT?" Rock yelled out.

"YO, YOU ROCK?" That question really put Rock on high alert, because nobody except Rena knew him by that name, and she was currently taking a shower. And it couldn't be Reek because Reek owned a Cadillac Escalade, and this car was a hupty. So Rock unholstered his Smith and Wesson 500 and cupped it behind his back.

This scene reminded him of when he first encountered Reek's cousin, Sharif, on Central Avenue. Rock gripped his gun tighter and hoped that this scene didn't play out the same way. "WHO ASKING?" Rock responded.

Suddenly, Reek emerged from the driver's side.

Rock ran towards him intent on embracing his long, lost friend, however stopped short when Reek pulled out a burner on him. He back up slightly.

Rock followed Reek's fear ridden eyes to the gun that he was still holding in his hands. In his excitement he totally forgot about it.

Rock stood halfway off halfway on the curb with a hurt look on his face. He put his gun away, then put his hands up as if stopping traffic. He then began walking slowly towards Reek.

Reek continued to hold his gun. Sure Rock was his man; however it was a lot that his so-called man had to explain before they could move on. Like why he left him for dead on his living room floor. And why the police had found the burnt remains of his cousin and two other unidentified in his other house.

It doesn't take a genus to figure out that at least one of those unidentified corpses was Jacquie.

Damn, what caused Rock to kill his own bitch like that? Fire had to be one of the worse ways to go out. Rock must really have los this mind, Reek thought to himself.

"Reek, put down the gun. It's me . . . it's your boy Rock."

"I know who you are," Reek responded, with a distrustful look on his face.

"Reek, I'm so glad you alive. I really thought you was dead."

"Oh, you thought I was dead or wished I was dead?"

Reek's comment really hurt him to his heart. "Come on Reek, think, do you really think I would tell you where I was resting at if I wanted you dead? You know we don't handle business like that." Rock could see that Reek was really considering his last words.

Reek stuffed his gun back down the front of his jeans, then dapped his old friend. That still didn't let him off the hook in Reek's book. However, it did break the ice.

"You hungry?" Rock asked.

"Yeah, me and my man ain't eat shit all morning."

"Cool, jump in the whip with me and have yo man follow us. I know this banging ass spot a minute from here."

While Reek conferred with Peewee, Rock jumped in his Porcha nine eleven.

Reek's abrupt action of pulling out a gun, caused Rock to rethink his plans. At first, he had thought about inviting Reek to his room to talk and had even considered introducing him to his new girlfriend. However, since Reek pulled a gun out on him and since he was traveling with a nigga he didn't even know, Rock didn't trust it. So, he decided to take them to a public eatery far, far away from where he laid his head at.

He jumped in his car and watched them intently from the safety of his bulletproof tented windows.

When Reek finally jumped in, he pulled off and decided to jump on the highway.

He remembered passing many restaurants when Rena first brought him here and had decided to drive as long as it took to straighten things out with his boy. Besides he thought he might not get a better opportunity to talk to Reek alone.

The car was silent, each man entrenched in his own thoughts.

Rock went first. He decided that the cold hard truth was the best policy.

"I'm sorry I had to rock your cuzzen." Rock's words caught Reek by surprise. That wasn't the way he suspected Rock would open up the conversation.

Reek put his head down, then asked, "But why?"

"It just happened so fast. Your cuzzen was cool peoples. He even helped me out of a jam, but he shot Jacquie and I just couldn't handle that."

"He shot Jacquie?" Reek asked, while picking up his head with a look of utter surprise on his face.

"Yeah, blew her head clean off," Rock said with a cool calmness to his voice.

"A'ight, that cleaned that up, but it still don't explain why you left me for dead on your living room floor."

Now it was rock's turn to look surprised. "So, that's what you think, that I just left you there for dead?" Rock's voice cracked.

He put the car in cruise control, then turned towards Reek, making sure to catch eye contact.

"Reek, I love you. You, my boy. Had I known you was still alive I woulda took you to the hospital.

"Hopefully not to you might die," Reek spit jokingly. And with that they both broke out in laughter, because you might die was the hood nickname for U.M.D., United medical and Dentistry. The reason they called it you might die was because of its high mortality rate.

They both had known people who had gone to the hospital with something as simple as an asthma attack and would later on die form what U.M.D. would describe as complications.

Now that things seemed cool between them, Rock pulled off the highway and into the parking lot of IHOP.

Peewee followed close behind them with hand secured tightly on his gun, just in case his OG Reek gave him the word.

Once inside, Rock ordered a steak, cheese, eggs, and pancake platter for everybody.

"Yo Rock, this my man Peewee from off of Hawthorn and Clinton."

Rock stood up and shook Peewee's hand firmly. "Always nice to meet a fellow 'Brick City' native."

"Yeah, this the fast thinker I was telling you about that saved Big Nick's baby."

"Yeah, that's fucked up what happened to my man Nick, and he just came home too," Rock said with a sadness to his face.

"Word living in Newark like living in Afghan or some shit. Niggas hitting niggas with RPG's and roadside bombs and shit."

"That's true Reek, so what you wanna do now?" Rock was asking Reek in code if he had some drugs to sell and if so what type of drugs was it.

"Yeah, like I said before I heard through the grapevine that you was moving some girl heavy up here, so I decided to go all in on some boy."

Peewee was totally clueless throughout the entire conversation. Actually, when Reek talked about going all in on some boy, he thought he was talking some gay shit. Because the slang they used pre-dated him, he had no idea that they were discussing cocaine and heroin the whole time.

"Well, I'ma Hoffa at my peoples and see if we could make it happen for you. In the meantime between time we gotta find you a spot to crash."

"Already taken care of big homey. We copped some rooms on the way over here."

"Still, I'm glad to see you Reek. As a matter fact, we going out tonight to celebrate the reunion of the dynamic hustling dual."

"Do you think that's wise big homey?" Reek asked with genuine concern on his face.

"Listen, my jump-off from up here. I'm sure she gotta low key club we could hit up . . . besides I gotta introduce you to my peoples and see if you could get rid of that boy." Rock paid the bill and prepared to leave.

"So what time you wanna head out for the club?" Reek asked while putting on his coat.

"Around ten o'clock. That give me enough time to hoffa at my peoples," Rock answered while dapping and hugging Reek.

Back in the car Peewee asked Reek about the conversation that him and Rock had at the table, and he broke out in hysterical laughter.

As soon as he wiped the tears out of his eyes, he explained to his young hustler that girl was old school for cocaine and boy was code for heroin.

"So tonight we going meet up with Rock's peoples to see if we could knock off that work?"

"Yeah, Peewee and I hope it works out because boy, I mean diesel could go bad in a week, but as long as we keep it in something dry like rice or oatmeal it could last for a good two months.

"So that's why you bought all that rice for. At first I thought you was about to open up a Chinese restaurant."

"Hah, haaah real funny. I know one thing that you won't find so funny, if we can't get rid of this dope, we going be in some deep shit.

"So I guess you and your man cool now?" Peewee asked with a look of genuine concern on his young face.

"Yeah, we cool. He explained what happened. I knew something serious had to go down for Rock to kill my cuzzin . . . he really not the type of dude that just be popping niggas for nothing."

"Yeah, he don't really seem like that type of dude," Peewee agreed, but still planned to keep an eye on him. Them old school niggas was slick, and Rock seemed like he been around for a while.

Rock returned to his hotel room, feeling excited that his man Reek was still alive. However, he still couldn't shake that uneasy feeling that something bad was about to happen.

He looked at Rena. She was laying on the bed filing her nails. When she finally noticed him, she rolled her eyes.

"So, now you mad at me?" Rock asked, but Rena didn't respond. She just continued to do her nails as if he wasn't even there.

Rock went to her and kissed her gently about her neck and cheek.

"Stooooop," Rena whined, while turning away and grinning.

"Baby, I tried to tell you when you was in the shower that I was stepping out to Hoffa at my man Reek."

"The one that died?"

"Yeah baby. Come to find out that nigga still alive and we all going out to celebrate."

"TONIGHT, I GOTTA GET READY." Rena jumped up with excitement and ran over to the closet, surveying the clothes that he had recently purchased for her. She couldn't wait for a special occasion to bust out with her new duds, and finally that day had come.

She turned around showcasing a short, lacy black and red Fendi dress. "You like this one?" she asked while smiling at him.

Rock nodded his approval, then lit up a pre-rolled weed blunt, and watched Rena's soft ass bounce seductively as she hummed a JAY-Z song and danced to her own rhythm.

Before leaving, Rock called his cousins and told them to meet him at Club Paradise and to bring a tester for Reek's heroin.

Rock and Rena stepped out of their room looking like they was walking down the red carpet at the Source Awards.

It was Friday night. The parking area was filled with the activity of men and women of all creeds and colors, happy to finally take their two-day vacation from work.

Everybody was paid except for Rock. He was still waiting on the money from the two kilos he just gave to his cousins.

Usually he would be going out on the town with a pocketful of money. However, since he was on the run, he wasn't able to collect any money from his legitimate businesses back home.

He rarely touched any of his flip money, especially for something as remedial as going out to the club. So, this night he only had five hundred bucks on him. Still, Rena and Rock looked like they had a million dollars.

Rena, Rock, Peewee, Reek, the twins and their tester all met up in the parking lot of Club Paradise, prior to going in.

"Ah baby is it cool if I got in with my burner?" Rock asked as soon as he saw they had to step through a metal detector. Rena put her hand in his and assured him that he would be alright.

When they got to the detector, she gave the bouncers a wink and a head nod, and not only did they not have to go through the metal detector, but they didn't get searched either.

The other party goers stared at them with amazement and confusion on their faces. For the most part getting into Club Paradise was like getting into a visiting room in Federal Prison. The surrounding neighborhood was so bad that the club owners spent extra money on security to better protect their patrons.

The atmosphere of the club was wild and loud, just the way Rock liked it. It was dark and packed with men and women of all ages, colors and creeds. Big butt country girls dragged their men on the dance floor, dropped down and got their eagle on.

The D.J. was spinning the latest U.G.K. record and the whole club went crazy with excitement.

Rock and his team found the darkest corner of the place, sat down and ordered drinks.

"ROCK, THIS MY MAN BUGALUE. HE GOING BE TESTING THAT DOG FOOD FOR YOU," Keith yelled in his ear between sips of Belvi. Peewee gave him a small package stamped BAD COMPANY, and Bugalue took off in the direction of the bathroom. When he returned several minutes later, his eyes was a glassy yellowish color. He gave them the thumbs up, then went back out to the dance floor and did the dope fiend shuffle.

While everybody else mingled and partied, Rock sat alone nursing a cognac, taking in the whole scene and thinking about the future.

Though everything was going good at the moment, he knew that when it came to the drug game there was no guarantees. All the money, drugs, cars and girls he had today could be gone tomorrow. All the people you had to step on to get to the top, you're going to meet on the way back down.

After leaving the club, everybody once again met up near rock's Porsche to discuss plans.

******

Meanwhile, after three days of recovery, Bree decided to hit the club in search of robbery victims.

Robbing wasn't really his forte, but since Lanceen had pistol whipped him, took all of his work and most of his money, Bree had a lot to make up for.

He was so upset that he got beaten up and robbed by a girl, that the only plan he could formulate was to stick up a couple of niggas. He hoped the fact that he was caught slipping and by a girl, didn't get out in the hood. Besides, he had a reputation to uphold.

Since he didn't have much money, he decided to forego the club festivities, and lay low in the parking lot. He really wanted to kill that bitch Lanceen, but that would come later—business before pleasure.

Bree spotted the twins in a small crowd.

It finally dawned on him; Kevin was responsible for that bitch robbing him. He wanted to get him back for stiffing him on that kilo, so he sent his bitch at him. It was all finally coming to him. Lanceen was Kevin's girlfriend. Why else would she be sucking him off like that in front of his house. Yeah, Bree was watching the whole thing. Kevin bussed twice in her mouth, then stole his kilo sale.

That was the last straw. Bree was furious beyond control.

He took his borrowed TECH-9 and attempted to creep up on them for a better shot. If Kevin tried to run, he would just have to shoot through the crowd to get him, Bree reasoned.

He crouched down and made his way between a group of parked cars, stopping only when threatened to be discovered. Damn, only six cars separated him from his victim. Who by the way seemed to have grown in number. It didn't look like that many people when he first spotted them. Now it looked like a bachelor's party. Oh well, they all could get it.

He slowly released the safety and cocked his gun. When he did so, he noticed the tall one look up from what looked like a very intense conversation. Did he hear that?

Bree put his ears towards the group and noticed that they did in fact stop talking. He slowly eased his head towards the surface of a parked old school Buick Regal, and locked eyes with Rock. Apparently, he had told everybody else to scatter, because the crowd started to taper off in opposite directions.

Fuck it, it was now or never, Bree thought to himself as he stood up and began to fire recklessly into the crowd. Everybody in the parking lot ran for cover, including the tall man who had first spotted him. He tried to keep an eye on him, however, he seemed to disappear in the dimly lit parking area.

He crouched back down only to reload. He was nervous and sweating profusely. Out of all that shooting he didn't seem to hit a thing.

Now that his night was wasted, his next step was escape. Bree was sure that all that gunfire didn't go unnoticed by the cops, and he didn't want to stick around to answer questions. Making his way between cars, he began the daunting task of retreat.

Once he made it safely back to his car, he tucked his gun under his coat, then nervously fumbled with his car keys, dropping them to the ground. "Damn!"

BOCK! BOCK! BOCK! The bullets from Rock's gun whizzed by him, missing his head by mere inches. Had it not been for him dropping his car keys, he probably be dead right now. He was taking on gunfire from multiple angles. While Rock was on one side shooting at him, Peewee and Reek was on the other.

Rock began maneuvering around cars, trying to get a better shot.

Bree stood up and returned fire on Peewee and Reek. It was crunch time, fight or flight, and Bree wasn't about to go out like no sucker. They ducked down just in time and the TECH-9's bullets struck the side of the car.

Several more cars and I got him, Rock thought to himself.

Meanwhile, shooting back bought Bree the time he needed to get his car door opened. He took a deep breath, gunned the engine and the car bolted out the parking space and onto the road.

Rock ran to the middle of the parking lot and emptied his gun into Bree's back window, shattering it to pieces.

He ran past the spot where Bree had just been and saw the remains of what could've been a bad night for them all. As he made it back to his car, he thanked GOD that the shells was laying on the ground instead of him.

His heart was beating fast. No matter how many shootouts he been involve din, they never seemed to get easier.

Rock started his car and thought of pursuing the unknown assailant, then thought better of it, knowing that that bastard was gone. Instead, he called everybody's cells and arranged a meeting at the twin's house.

Rena was visibly shaken. Her teeth chattered audibly, like she was trapped naked in a freezing cold icehouse. She was entrenched in her own thoughts. She couldn't believe that she had to go to Kevin's house and no doubt after a shootout.

Her plans to avoid Kevin had worked perfectly up until now. Now she had to meet up with him at his house. This truly was becoming the worse night of her life. It ranked right up there with the night she had to stab her own father to death for raping her all them years. That thought put a slight smile on her face, knowing that her father would never violate anybody else where he was at.

Maybe she could ask Rock if she could wait in the car while he handled his business. She looked over at him. His face was a stonewall. She thought better of asking him to stay in the car, especially after the shootout. Rock was now on high alert, and she never would leave his sight now. He was already extremely overprotective of her, but she loved that about him. It made her feel wanted.

Rock could feel her staring at him from the passenger seat. However, reluctantly ignored her. He had bigger things to worry about, like why a nigga he didn't even know, in a town he wasn't even known in, just tried to take them out.

Rock concluded that this beef couldn't have had anything to do with him, at least not directly. His sixth sense was right. He knew something bad was to become of that night. He just didn't expect a nigga would be shooting at him.

As he drove, he briefly relived the whole shootout. He couldn't believe how reckless that nigga was with that gun. He shot with a total disregard for the value of human life.

Rock didn't know exactly what they should do next, but he knew something had to happen and fast if they was to continue doing business in this town.

North Carolina was just like any other hood. Once the word got out that niggas had shot at them with impunity, it would be open season. And Rock refused to look weak in front of his team or have his team misrepresenting him.

They all piled into the living room of the twin's condo.

Rock took up his regular seat on the Lazy Boy, while everybody else took whatever seats were available on the couch.

The entire room was completely silent. So silent that you could hear a rat piss on cotton. Everybody was waiting for Rock to speak.

"So what we going do about this shit?" he asked while waving Rena over to sit on his lap.

"We going murk this nigga," Reek chimed in

"But first we need to find out who was shooting at us and why."

"FUCK WHO HE WAS. WE GOTTA TAKE ACTION NOW!" Kevin said with anger in his voice.

"We definitely going take action, but we want to be strategic when we do and we want to make sure that this shit never happen again," Rock paused then continued, "so did anybody recognize that nigga?" He looked across the room and everybody nodded no, in response.

"Well, maybe I can help." The voice sounded real familiar to Rock, however it wasn't coming from anybody he had been with that night.

In the split second between action and reaction the thought process takes place. And a lot of thoughts was going through Rock's head when he heard that voice. Before turning to the direction of the sound, he dug deeply into his memory database in an attempt to recognize the female voice.

The firs thing that came to mind was Lanceen, however logic suggested that it would have been impossible for her to be there. *Besides, how could she be there*, Rock thought, *when she didn't even know where he was.*

The last time he saw Lanceen he was diving out of her back window, trying to escape the police. No, that voice couldn't possibly belong to Lanceen. He looked over his left shoulder only to find that his logic had deceived him. The voice that he heard was hers.

His heart skipped a beat. Things couldn't get any worse. Here he was sitting with the woman he loved and staring into the eyes of the woman he fucked.

His past and his future was sitting in the same room at the same time. He braced himself, waiting for a nuclear explosion. Rock hoped like hell that his past didn't reveal their love affair to his future wife.

When Lanceen went over to Kevin and passionately kissed him on the lips, Rock's heart went back to normal.

"Hey, don't I know you?" Reek asked, recognizing Lanceen from the part back home.

Rock spoke up, "Nah Reek, that's not who you think it is. That was somebody else."

"Nah Rock, I'm pretty sure. I never forget a face, especially one as pretty as hers."

Rock gave Reek the signal to drop it, then changed the subject. "So, you said you could hep?"

"Yes," Lanceen replied. "But first let me introduce myself. My name is Lanceen Howard Diggs and I work for the Federal Bureau of Investigation back in Newark, New Jersey."

Everybody except for Rock busted out in laughter.

"THAT'S ... HA ... HAAA ... HA MY BABY MS. L ALWAYS KNOW WHEN TO BUS OUT WITH A GOOD JOKE," Kevin yelled while clutching his stomach.

Once Lanceen pulled out her badge, Bugalue got nervous. As a cold-hearted dope fiend, he was no stranger to arrest. Bugalue had been arrested enough times to know the difference between a fake badge and a real one, and the one that was being held by Lanceen sure looked authentic to him.

Rock felt betrayed as he slowly eased his hand into his inside coat pocket and clutched his hammer.

"Don't look at me like that Maleek," Lanceen said.

To Rock, her words solidified that she was truly a F.B.I. Agent because not many people knew his real name. The only question now was why had she gone through so much trouble just to get to him?

"I know you feel betrayed Maleek, however, kindly remove your hand away from your inside coat pocket. Besides, you wouldn't want to kill your baby anyway," Lanceen said with a smirk on her face and a Glock nine in her hands.

She pointed her gun directly at Rena's face. "You, Miss Chocolate drop, kindly remove your funky ass off my man's lap and move over to the wall." Rena nervously did as she was told, while Reek attempted to reach for his gun.

"I wouldn't do that if I was you unless you wanna taste your friend's brains all over your lips," Lanceen said while pressing her weapon against Rock's temple. "In fact, I want all you against the wall." When nobody moved, Lanceen yelled, "NOW!"

Everybody except Rock put their hands up, then stood up and faced the wall.

"You too lover boy."

Rock reluctantly got up and joined the others.

Lanceen quickly grabbed a pillowcase, searched the group, then placed their guns into it. When she searched Rock, she made sure to pay special attention to his genital area. Lanceen openly fondled him against the wall. However, Rock's mind was far from sex. He was too busy thinking about the slim possibility that Lanceen was pregnant by him.

He reminisced about the two brief sexual encounters he had with her and remembered that he didn't bus in either occasion. However, he was remotely aware that it was possible that she could have gotten pregnant by his pre-cum.

He looked towards Rena and noticed she was furious.

"Maleek, you come back here with me. EVERYBODY ELSE STAY ON THE WALL," Lanceen demanded.

Rock walked her to the kitchen and they both sat down and just stared at each other. He could see that Lanceen had been truly hurt by him.

She spoke in a whisper, "So, I see you the type of guy that never finishes what he starts."

When those words came out of her mouth, Rock felt relieved. He now knew that Lanceen's intention was not to lock him up.

He looked at her posture and noticed that she even lowered her gun.

Rock chose his next words carefully, knowing that what he said could be the difference between freedom or jail or life and death for them all.

"I always finish what I start," Rock said while making the daring move to lean in for a kiss. He didn't know if it would work or not, but nothing beats a failure like a try. To his surprise, Lanceen kissed him back, and even closed her eyes and slid her tongue into his mouth.

Rock surveyed the room while kissing Lanceen, and could see a lone tear grace Rena's cheek, as she turned away from him and back to the wall disguised. He felt bad for her and hoped that she understood that he was sacrificing himself for the greater good of the team.

He gently took Lanceen by her hand and led her to Rena's room.

"What about them?" she questioned.

"Let me worry about that," Rock spoke over his shoulder, then added, "You'll chill in there, I'll take care of this." He smacked Lanceen hard on her ass all at the same time. She winced with excitement.

While Rock was in the room with Lanceen, everybody else relaxed and talked in low tones.

"What you think he in there doing with her?" Rena questioned.

"What you think he in there doing . . . he fucking my bitch," Kevin responded with anger.

Rena buried her face in her hands and cried silently.

Meanwhile, Rock was in the other room giving Lanceen the fuck of her life. He literally had her attempting to climb the walls.

Though she was royally enjoying herself, Rock wasn't. He viewed the entire sexual experience like a job. He knew that in spite of himself he had to be at peek performance. The freedom of himself and his family hung in the balance.

Lanceen made sure to moan loud enough for that chocolate bitch in the next room could hear. Rock was hers and she had to mark her territory. If Lanceen could have pissed on him and gotten away with it, she would have. She wanted to make sure that Rena knew that he belonged to her, and that she could have him whenever she pleased.

Rock took her from the back long stroking her while smacking her hard on the ass with total disregard for the small life she was carrying. He wanted to punish her for all the bullshit she'd caused them. Lanceen felt his stiff wood in her stomach, but ignored it, enjoying every inch of his punishment.

Afterwards, they laid back on the bed, talked and shared a Newport.

"So, did I earn my gun back?"

"Maybe," Lanceen teased, with a girlish grin on her face.

The power of the dick was unmatched, Rock thought to himself.

"Agent Lanceen, let me ask you a more serious question. How come I'm not locked up right now?" Rock sat up on the bed and looked her square in the eyes, then continued, "I mean obviously you had to be investigating me back in New Jeru, and since you the Feds I'm sure you already know I'm on the run."

Lanceen nodded her head in agreement.

"And on top of all that," Rock continued, "I'm sure that what we just did wasn't standard arrest procedures."

She playfully kissed him on the cheek, "Yes, all that's true. I was assigned to investigate you on racketeering, extortion, murder, and drug distribution."

She passed the cigarette back to him and he finished it off and put it out.

"But I didn't know that I would fall in love with you or get pregnant by you," Lanceen whispered, then put her head down.

Rock had to admit that he did like the vulnerable more softer side of Lanceen, but he had to stay focused on the task at hand, protecting himself and the family that he had left in the next room.

He knew that if they were to survive this, he would have to run the tightest game that he had. He'd already seduced her boy, now he had to seduce the most important part of her, her mind. Some say that women are built like a pyramid from top to bottom, so with that if you could capture a woman's mind then her body has to follow.

He put his arms around her and cradled her like a newborn baby.

"I was feeling you too ma." He gently picked her head up and made her face him. "So, tell me what we going do now?" Rock was stalling for time. He hoped that by the time they emerged from the room everybody, including the drugs would be gone.

"What you mean what I'm going do now? I want us to be a family."

Apparently, this girl was delusional, he thought to himself. There was no way he could ever bring himself to be with a Federal Agent, baby or no baby. However, instead of revealing his true feelings, he decided to humor her and see how much information he could get.

"And what we going do about Rena?"

Lanceen's face turned beet red with anger. She was jealous. She couldn't understand what he saw in that dark skinned bitch in the first place.

Rena didn't seem like much to look at to her. Sure she had a little ass and hips, but nothing compared to what she was holding, which by the way was starting to get a little out of control because of the baby. Suddenly, she felt subconscious about her figure and the stretch marks that plagued the surface of her stomach like a road map. She attempted, unsuccessfully, to cover it with her small hands.

This was all his fault. Had he not seduced her with his magic dick none of this would have ever happened.

Lanceen's emotions was bouncing all over the place. She went from love to anger, to shame, then back to anger.

Finally she said, "We going kill that bitch."

Rock was shocked by her words, however, he refused to show it. Instead, he wisely decided to play it cool.

He took in a deep breath of air and thought fast. "We can't do that right now."

"And why not?" Lanceen demanded.

"Cause right now I need that bitch to help me operate my drug business. You know I'm hot."

As much as she hated to, she had to admit that he was right. He was hot and the best thing for him to do was to lay low. But why couldn't she replace Rena? Besides, who would have a better inside track than a Federal Agent. However, when she expressed her thoughts, Rock immediately shut her down, claiming his cousins wouldn't feel comfortable having to report to a F.B.I. Agent.

After a couple of minutes of going back and forth on the subject, Lanceen finally gave in, but made rock promise that when the time came she would be the one to end Rena's life.

When Rock and Lanceen finally emerged from the back room, everybody was gone, at least all except for Reek. He was sitting on the couch patiently waiting with the twins Berrat M468, that Rock had given them, along with their last package of work.

When he saw Lanceen he casually aimed the semi-automatic rifle at her.

Rock was relieved that his plan had worked. He had kept her occupied long enough for everybody to get away. However, seeing Reek there pointing a gun at Lanceen was an unexpected twist.

He relished in the fact that he was back in control, but in the back of his mind he knew that if they was to make it out of this one, he had to give Lanceen the illusion that she was the one actually in control.

"Reek, I don't think that will be necessary anymore," Rock said while winking his eye at him. "My Boo has worked all the bugs out and told me she was going keep us posted if she heard anything about a riad or somen, so we could turn it all the way up."

Lanceen looked at him with confusion in her eyes. He had never discussed no such deal with her. She was about to protest until Rock walked over to Reek and gently removed the gun from his hand, then winked at her.

"Lanceen's a part of our family now," Rock said.

That's all Lanceen ever wanted from him, was to be a part of the family.

To her, things couldn't have gotten any better. The man that she loved accepted her as a Fed and had even promised to be a father to their unborn child. What more could she ask for?

"So baby you ready to go back to my room? I'm ready for round two." Lanceen crept behind him and wrapped her arms around his waist.

He turned around to face her, with pain in his eyes and face.

Lanceen could tell that whatever he had to say he really didn't want to, so she decided to relieve him of his duty. "I know, I know you got to go back with that bitch Rena."

"Unfortunately, yes," he said, then continued, "I'm sorry baby."

"No need to apologize. You got to do what you got to do."

Rock felt relieved that she didn't put up too big of a fight. This was going to be easier than he originally thought. Everything he wanted to say, Lanceen had already said it for him.

He wrapped her tightly in his arms. "That's what I love about you, you always know what I'm thinking."

"Hold on, hold on, I'm glad to hear that you love me, and I love you too, but," she pushed herself away from him then continued with her tirade. "If you fuck that bitch one more time, I'm going kill both you." and with that warning she left.

"Damn Rock, I knew I knew that chick."

"Yeah, but who would have guessed she was a fuckin' cop," Rock responded, then sat down exhausted.

"So what you think we should do?"

"I don't know yet Reek, but we gotta figure somen out . . . by the way where everybody go?" Rock asked.

"Oh, I sent them out with that work. I didn't see a need for all to get bagged. Besides, I didn't want them around just in case you wanted to handle that Fed situation a lil bit differently."

"Well I guess I better do my ritual so I could think this shit through."

"Yo Rock, before you got hit the tub, tell me how it was hitting that Fed?"

"It was like fucking a pig," Rock said over his shoulder as he headed for the bathroom.

He prepared his bath water, however before jumping in, he decided to call everybody, starting off with his cousins.

"What's up? You alright?"

"We cool," Keith answered. "When you went in the room with shorty, Reek had us get rid of the work."

"That's what's up, where you all at?"

"We on our way back from dropping Bugalue off. By the way he said that dog food was the shit."

"That's good money. Call Rena for me and tell her to be ready to go when she gets back," Rock said while taking off his shirt.

"Oh . . . yeah cuzz Rena not with us."

"WHAT YOU MEAN SHE NOT WITH YOU ALL?" Rock asked, finding himself yelling into the receiver.

"Yeah, cuzz she was listening at the door when you was handling your business with that shorty . . . and when we got outside, she took off crying."

"AND YOU DIDN'T FOLLOW HER?"

"We tried, but she started causing a scene and we got all this work in the car."

Though Rock was upset he had to admit that they had done all they could.

He put his shirt back on and ran out of the house. When he got to the parking lot, Reek was right behind him breathing heavily.

Chapter 15

"What happen?" Reek asked with the M468 in his hands.

At the same moment the Sheriff that lived next door, drove by. Rock and Reek were oblivious to his presence. However, he wasn't to theirs.

He saw the big gun in the young man's hand, but neglected to call it in. Besides, it wasn't actually a crime in North Carolina to walk outside with a gun. It was hunting season. However, the Sheriff did decide he'd keep an eye on them.

"Reek, let me get that hammer. I'm gong to see if I could find Rena."

"You want me and Peewee to go with you? He sitting right there in the car."

He looked in the direction where Reek was pointing in, and sure enough Peewee was there. But instead of waving at them, he looked like he was pointing at something himself.

Rock traced his fingers to the Sheriff's car, then tucked the big gun underneath his cot.

"Too late asshole," the Sheriff whispered to himself.

"You and Peewee meet me at my hotel room, I'm going find Rena."

Rock ran off, then stopped short. "Oh yeah, here's the key."

Reek took the key and they both parted ways.

It wasn't long before he caught up with Rena. On foot she'd only made it a short distance from the condo. Rock slowed the Porsche to a crawl and rolled the window down when he spotted her. "RENA!"

She looked directly at him, then turned around and kept on walking. "I DON'T WANT TO TALK TO YOU!" Rena yelled over her shoulder.

"RENA GET YO DIZZY ASS IN THE CAR BEFORE YOU CAUSE A SCENE!" Rock yelled, his patience running thin.

"CAUSE A SCENE . . . CAUSE A SCENE." Rena stopped in her tracks. "CAUSE A SCENE LIKE WHEN YOU WAS IN MY BEDROOM TRYING TO PUT THAT DIRTY BITCH HEAD THROUGH THE WALL."

Rock had to admit she had him on that one. "That was business baby, I did that for all of us."

"OH YEAH . . . THE WAY YOU WAS BOUNCING THAT BITCH HEAD OFF THE WALL IT SURE SEEMED LIKE PLEASURE TO ME."

"WELL, IT WASN'T. SO STOP RUNNING FROM YOUR PROBLEMS LIKE A LITTLE GIRL AND JUMP IN THE CAR AND HANDLE THEM."

She reluctantly jumped in the car.

Rock knew that his words would do the trick. His words stung Rena to the core.

They drove back to the condo in silence. He would have preferred to go back to his hotel room, however, because of the situation with Lanceen, he needed to collect whatever money his cousins had just in case him and Rena had to make a quick getaway. He also planned on paying a visit to Rena's safety deposit box to retrieve his money. The situation with Rena was kinda shaken so he really didn't trust her at the moment. Besides, if they had to get out of town in a hurry, they were going to need that money.

By the time they made it to the condo, the twins were already there. They could hear them arguing, even before they got to the door.

"SO WHAT HE OUR COUSIN . . . THAT DON'T MAKE IT RIGHT," Rock and Rena overheard Kevin saying.

"Trust me, he didn't want to fuck yo girl, especially the way he feeling Rena," Keith countered.

"Yeah, that was strike one, and Ms. L was strike two. There won't be another."

What the fuck was that supposed to mean, Rock asked himself, then put his ear back to the door.

"SO WHAT YOU GOING DO?" Keith questioned.

"I GOING KILL THAT NIGGA."

Rock heard enough. He had to get in there and defuse the situation as fast as possible. Had he known his day was going to go this bad he would have stayed in the house.

He tried the door and to his surprise it was unlocked.

"These niggas must be really slipping," he thought out loud.

"Baby can I wait in the car?" Rena asked politely.

He turned to her and saw distress in her face and eyes. He was surprised on how fast stress had aged her. Rena looked ten years older. Without saying a word he handed her his car keys and watched as she walked down the hallway with her head hung low.

He felt bad and promised himself that he'd find a way to make it up to her.

Rock took a deep breath, then walked in the living room.

When Kevin saw him, he shot at him. Had it not been for the quick action of Keith jerking and wrestling the gun away from his brother, the bullet would have struck Rock in the head instead of the wall panel beside him.

Everything just happened so fast that Rock didn't know what to think or do next. Usually he would have pulled out his gun and returned fire, however this wasn't a usual situation. This was a situation involving his flesh and blood cousin. The same cousin that he used to watch when he was younger, the same cousin that who used to wet the bed and with him in it. For GOD sake, he used to change this boys' diapers.

His betrayal and disloyalty caused Rock to upholster his gun and point it at his cousin. He felt like Cane betraying Abel, except in this case it was family against family all over a bitch that he cared nothing for.

Everything seemed to develop slow from that point on. Rock felt like he was having an outer body experience, like he was watching a movie of himself. He watched helplessly as his movie self, raised his gun and took aim at his little cousin. He next witnessed his movie self close its eyes and began to fire.

He wondered briefly why his movie self had closed its eyes and concluded that he didn't want to see the harm that was about to befall his flesh and blood cousin. However, he felt that the effort was futile, considering the fact that he could still see what was going on in spite of his movie self closing its eyes.

He could see the bullets rip through his cousin's arms and shoulders, missing their vital organs by mere inches. He watched as his twin cousins fell to the floor, clutching wounds in agony.

Rock's movie self was stuck in a daze. He just stood there with his eyes closed, firing on what was now an empty gun.

Soon after the shooting, a group of police officers crashed through the door and tackled him to the floor. The gun he was holding flew into the air and landed near the patio window. The cops cuffed everybody in the house, including the badly injured Keith and Kevin.

They reasoned that even though the twins were hurt, they still were dangerous. The cops considered them suspects in a shooting.

The police really didn't know what was going on. The only thing they knew was somebody was shooting, and in that general area. Had it not been for the quick action of an off-duty Sheriff that lived in the next building, they would have never found the shooters.

As Rock was being handcuffed and led out the door, his outer body experience ended. He was back in his body, and he hated what he saw next.

In the hallway there was pure pandemonium. EMT workers and police officers were running around in a frenzy. He wondered to himself what all the commotion as about. It wasn't until one of the officers jerked him to the side of the wall, that he realized what was going on. He helplessly watched as the Emergency medical Response Team carried a limp five-year-old boy out of the apartment next door.

He had been caught high above his left eye with a nine-millimeter round, while jumping up and down on his bed. The bullet that Keith had averted from Rock had found another target, an innocent child playing on his bed.

Rena watched helplessly undercover of Rock's Porsche, as her man and his twin cousins were roughly escorted away in handcuffs. Sure a part of her wanted revenge on Rock for fucking Lanceen, however jail was a place she wouldn't have wished on her worst enemy.

She had to fight the overwhelming urge to run out in the streets with tears in her eyes and be with her man. But she knew that she couldn't help him if they both were behind bars. No, she had to maintain a level head, and make sure she was ready to move whenever he called her.

When the cops left with Rock, she followed closely behind them. She wanted to know exactly where they were taking her man.

Her ride to the police station was a long one, and Rena was fighting the urge not to fall asleep at the wheel. She turned the music up and smacked herself repeatedly, in an attempt to fight off the ill effects of the alcohol she'd consumed earlier.

Once she found out where Rock was going to be held, she took off for the hotel. As she drove, she decided to play Rock's favorite album MACKAVELLI. She didn't know why she did it, maybe it was because 2PAC reminded her of her own man.

She looked on the passenger seat and was excited to find that Rock had left his black leather jacket. She snatched it from the seat, then put it on as fast as she could. His scent comforted her. And even though his jacket was way too big for her, the leather felt like a protective glove.

Back at the hotel room she woke up the next morning, still wrapped up in his jacket. She had a banging headache from drinking the night before.

"Baby could you please pass me an aspirin out of the bathroom," Rena asked Rock.

When she didn't receive a response, she became highly upset. She couldn't believe that this nigga couldn't even get her an aspirin, especially after she cheated on her with that cop bitch. Rena was appalled.

She tried again, this time yelled at him even louder, "ROCK COULD YOU PLEASE GET ME A GODDAMN ASPIRIN PLEASE!"

It took her a while to realize that she was actually alone. Rock was locked up.

She briefly closed her eyes and the horrible memory of the night before flooded back into her mind like the Jersey shore after that 2013 hurricane.

Chapter 16

Meanwhile, Rock was going through the booking process in the County Jail.

"BEND OVER AND CRACK A SMILE!" the officer yelled aggressively, pissed off that Rick wasn't cooperating.

Rock was naked and cold. The cops had cranked up the AC to a brisk twenty degrees. He felt degraded and humiliated having to first strip down, then bend over in front of a bunch of white officers who seemed to enjoy looking at men's asses.

He bent over, apparently not fast or far enough, because when he did, one of the officers kicked him in the ass, causing him to crash into the concrete wall in front of him.

"UGGGG SHIIIIT . . . WHAT THE FUCK YOU'LL DOING?" Rock protested.

"BOY WHEN I SAY CRACK A SMILE, I MEAN LET ME SEE THAT ASS!" one officer yelled while the others stayed back and laughed.

Rock wanted to get up and start swinging, however he knew that that's what they wanted. He reasoned that racism was a learned behavior. Besides, they were just upset because a little white boy got killed. And since he wasn't cooperating, they probably blamed him.

Rock spit, then got up and repeated the procedure, intent on getting this part of the booking process over.

He bent over, feeling as if he was taking the black race back four hundred years. The ignorant cops whistled and did cat calls behind him as they watched him.

After he was stripped of his dignity and manhood, he was tossed headfirst into a hard cell with nothing more than a flimsy hospital gown to protect his tropical body from the freezing cold.

"Maybe you could get some clothes after you's start cooperating nigga," the lead officer on the case whispered to him on his way past his cell.

Rock went to sleep balled up in the corner of his cell, still handcuffed.

When he woke up, he was thirsty and extremely hungry. "YO OFFICER, WHEN YOU'LL GOING DO CHOW?"

"SORRY NIGGA YOU MUSTA MISSED THAT!" he heard the hall officer respond.

"You dirty ass crackers," Rock whispered under his breath.

"WHAT WAS THAT BOY?"

Rock ignored him and thought about how he was going to get out of jail. *Truly this was no place for a black man,* he thought to himself.

"AH NIGGA... I MEAN MR. ROBERTS. YOU GOT A LAWYER VISIT," he heard an officer yell out.

They threw some county blues in his cell, and he dressed as quickly as he could.

"AHH CRACKA... I MEAN OFFICER. I'M READY!" Rock yelled, while standing by his door.

"Here's your boots," the cop said while reluctantly tossing his Timberlands in the cell.

"WHERE THE FUCK MY SHOESTRINGS?"

"We kept them ... we wouldn't want you to hang it up before you get the electric chair for killing that nice white boy," he replied with a murderous look in his fat blue eyes.

Why they keep saying I murder that little kid, Rock asked to himself.

He stepped out the cell, looking confused.

They took him to the lobby, via elevator, then down a long corridor, finally into a small, cramped room. His lawyer was sitting comfortably behind a desk, patiently awaiting his arrival.

Rock's lawyer was freakishly slender, white, with a pair of gold wire-framed glassed on his face. He reminded him of Mr. Burns from off the Simpsons.

"Kindly release those shackles from my client," he said while glaring at the officers.

The men reluctantly complied with the lawyer's demands, then stood there as if they were standing guard.

"Gentlemen, if you will excuse us. There is a matter of client lawyer privilege," Rock's lawyer said sternly.

The men got the hint, and exited the room, leaving the door open.

"You can close that Mr. Roberts."

Rock closed the door, then sat down in the cold metal chair located in front of the lawyer's desk.

"Listen . . . no disrespect, but I don't need no crackpot Public Defender repre . . ."

The lawyer cut him off. "I assure you Mr. Roberts that I am no crackpot lawyer. My name is Mr. Windthropp. I work in one of the biggest firms in North Carolina and I was retained by your friend, a Mr. Reek this morning."

He shuffled a stack of papers in front of him then continued, "Whom by the way retained me on a payment plan."

"Okay, what we looking at here. Them cops said something 'bout they charging me for that little boy that got shot."

"It's a little early for discovery, but from what I gather from the police report it seems you are in fact being charged with murder," Windthropp said while handing him a copy of his police report.

Rock read it quickly, then screamed, "THIS SOME BULLSHIT!"

"Please calm down Mr. Roberts."

"CALM DOWN . . . CALM DOWN. WHAT THE FUCK YOU MEAN I DIDN'T KILL THAT BOY."

"Mr. Roberts I cannot help you if you don't calm down," he said calmly.

"IS EVERYTHING ALRIGHT IN THERE?" somebody yelled through the door.

"Yes, fine officer," Windthropp replied.

"How they going charge me with this shit?" rock asked feeling more confused now than he did before.

"If I had to guess, I'd say somebody was talking," his lawyer said honestly.

"Who could be talking? I was only locked up with my two cous . . ." Rock's own words answered his question.

"I'll talk to you when I have more information. Until then I advise you not to talk to anybody about your case," Windthropp said, then stood up indicating their meeting was ended.

As he walked back to his cell, he saw a dude from Philadelphia washing his clothes out in the toilet. He cringed, thinking about what his people had been reduced to.

The jury trial and sentencing all went quickly. He was given an all-white jury who had easily found him guilty of Criminal Racketeering, Drug Manufacturing, three counts of Manslaughter from his Jersey beef, and Second-Degree Murder for the child that got shot.

The Feds really didn't have much on him. It wasn't until his jealous rat of a cousin Kevin had turned States witness in exchange for a Nollo Pros (non prosecution) in the murder of the neighbor's five-year-old son.

Rock was Kevin's get-out-of-jail free card. And when he took the stand he gave an Emmy worthy performance, complete with crocodile tears and all.

He told the jury that Rock forced him and his twin brother to sell drugs for them, and how they had a rough time growing up in the hood, and the jury ate it up.

Mr. Windthropp fought like a World War II veteran. However, it was no match for the deceptive stratagem of the Federal Prosecutor.

Keith didn't testify at all, and only got five months in County for his involvement in all of this.

After the trial, Rock attempted to contact Rena on many occasions, but she wouldn't answer any of his phone calls. It wasn't until his sentencing that she finally showed up.

The sixty to a hundred twenty years didn't hurt him as bad as seeing Rena show up pregnant and holding hands with the one man responsible for his woes—snake ass rat ass Kevin. It took several sheriffs and the police to restrain Rock from attempting to murder Rena and his cousin.

After sentencing he made a mental note to tell Reek to finish them both off.

Good old Reek. Rock was so glad he had someone like him to depend on. Reek kept him posted on everything that was going on in the streets, except the news about Kevin and Rena moving in together and using his safety deposit money to do it.

Reek wanted to exact revenge for his man Rock, however the Feds were watching Kevin and Rena like a hawk. Rock was glad that Reek got to his storage unit work before Rena and Kevin did, otherwise that too would have been out for the taking.

He still had seven kilos of coke left and with that Rock could accomplish a lot from the inside.

He settled into his cell at SCI-Favette Prison. The days were long there, and he hoped that the Feds would have left him in North Carolina instead of transferring him to Pennsylvania. He was sent there on a short basis, until New Jersey could claim him.

Rock was miserable, until one day he looked into the kitchen window and saw a white woman with the biggest titties he'd ever seen in his life.

"YO . . . YO, HOMEBOY YOU EATING OR WHAT?" the CO yelled behind him.

Mesmerized by the massive size of the woman's breast, Rock had been holding up the meal line for over five minutes. Before moving on, he briefly looked into the woman's brown eyes, and to his surprise she smiled and waved at him, even though seconds ago his eyes were glued to her bodacious knockers.

The whole scene baffled him. All of his life he'd never been turned on by a white woman. In fact, he'd never even gotten close enough to one to know whether or not white women turned him on.

Since his hometown of Newark was predominantly black, the only time Rock encountered white people was either on TV or whenever he had to see a Judge. Besides that Rock really didn't know much about them.

"Yo CO how I get a job in the kitchen?"

The office ignored him at first. However, after he'd gotten his tray and sat down the cop came over. "If you want to get a job in the kitchen you have to write a request to Inmate Employment and to the kitchen supervisor."

"How long will it take them to get back at me?" Rock asked as the officer was walking away.

"Oh, you should be down there in a couple days," the cop responded, winked at him, then returned to his duties.

Rock attempted to go back to his meal, but every time he looked at his plate, he envisioned the white girl's hug melons. He tried to shake it off, but the vision just kept coming back. The meatballs, potatoes, even the green peas looked like titties to him.

When he made it back to the block, he put his request slip in immediately, and put it in the box for the kitchen job.

Two weeks later he was working.

Almost instantly all the white women on his shift noticed him. They admired him mostly for his height and dark, smooth complexion.

He was assigned to work line five. To his surprise, when he arrived there, the whole reason that he'd signed up for that lame job was staring him right in the face.

"Good morning," she said while extending her hand. Rock gently grabbed it and held on to it longer than needed.

"Good morning beautiful," he replied, while staring at her breast.

"What's your name?"

"Oh, my bag, my name Maleek, but most people call me Rock."

"Why they call you that, because you're rock hard?" the woman said while seductively licking her lips.

The sudden come on threw Rock for a loop. However, he knew that first expressions were everything, so he humored her.

"All the time," he replied, returning the seductive gesture.

Once other convicts filled the work area, the young woman named Ms. Bryan took him by the hand and led him to a spot near the window counter.

"Today you'll be with me."

"That sounds good to me," he countered.

She smiled, then continued, "I mean to learn the job."

She playfully slapped him on the arm, "Tomorrow you'll start work."

They conversed the entire time, while the other convicts shot him dirty looks.

Rock was amazed on how much he would have in common with a white girl from Pittsburg. He could now see why seventy percentage of married black men were married to white women, because they were so easy to get along with.

Rock shook those thoughts off, reasoning that no matter how demanding, argumentative black women were, he could never completely give up on them, even after getting betrayed by love twice in one year.

That night, before going to bed, he reflected on the last six months of his life.

He was well on his way form retiring from the game prior to getting locked up. He went from thousands of dollars a day to nineteen cents an hour. The game was just like Kya said, untrustworthy.

However, Rock was down but not out. He still had seven keys that his boy Reek was turning into cash as he thought.

He did the math and realized that his product was worth at least three hundred and fifty-two thousand dollars. And since Reek promised to get all his money for him, that increased his chances of getting out of prison. However, the appeal process was not for him. He had no faith in the system; besides he knew the Feds had him booked solid. With his own cousin turning witness against him, his chances of getting out on appeal was slim at best.

From that moment on, Rock knew what he had to do to get back out.

The next day he put his plan into action. He started holding secret meetings with other convicts and discussing how racist the guards acted towards black men in general. The white officers treated the black men in prison with total disrespect and the jail was a powder keg ready to go up. All he had to do was provide a small spark.

As the days turned into weeks and the weeks turned into months, Rock's small group of black power enthusiasts grew so large that he had to start holding meetings in the main yard.

"YEAH ROCK, JUST LAST WEEK THEM CRACKA'S JUMPED ON THAT OLD HEAD FOR NOTHING!" one of his devoted followers yelled out. The young man was referring to an incident that happened outside of one of the chow halls, when an older black man refused to obey a direct order and the guards jumped him, restrained him, then dragged him to the hole on his face, leaving a trail of blood and tissue in his wake. The scene reminded Rock of the yellow brick road except this road wasn't paved with bricks. It was paved with the blood, tears and facial tissue of an elderly black man.

"YEAH, THAT'S THE PROBLEM RIGHT THERE . . . THESE CRACKA'S DON'T RESPECT THE TRUE POWER OF THE BLACK MAN. OUR ANCESTORS WAS KINGS AND QUEENS!" Rock paused, then continued, "OUR PROUD PEOPLE BUILT THE PYRAMIDS AND THESE DEVILS TRY TO SAY THE ALIENS CAME DOWN AND BUILT IT, JUST BECAUSE THEY CAN'T TAKE THE CREDIT FOR IT!

"HELL, THEY EVEN TRIED TO CHOP THE NOSE OFF THE SPHINX, JUST ERASE OUR PROUD HISTORY." Rock stood up in the middle of a group of fifty angry black men that seemed to grow angrier and larger with his every word.

He felt like Malcolm X, running around the streets of Harlem, preaching the black power movement under the Nation.

At the height of his speech, Rock was politely interrupted by a lone guard. He was short and white.

"Excuse me sir, but . . . could you guys please break this crowd up a little bit. My Lieutenant getting on my ass about you'll group."

This was rock's chance to start a riot. Even though he felt bad for using this particular C/O the catalyst in which to complete his plans, because he kind of liked him. He just couldn't pass up such an opportunity.

Rock knew he had to really play his role now. The other men turned to the guard, then back to him, just waiting for his response. And Rock gave them one, "WHAT THE FUCK YOU MEAN YOU PEOPLE?"

"I . . . I, I didn't mean it like . . ."

Rock cut him off, "YES YOU DID. EVERY TIME YOU'LL SEE A GROUP OF BLACK MEN GATHERING UP, IT'S ALWAYS A PROBLEM."

He pointed to a small group of white boys, then continued, "I DON'T SEE YOU'LL SAYING SHIT TO THEM CRACKA'S STANDING OVER THERE!"

"YEAH, WHY YOU'LL AIN'T SAYING NOTHING TO DEEM?" one of the men asked.

"YEAH!" another one joined in.

The small guard began to slowly back away from the mob. When a couple men started waling towards him, he hit his panic button. Suddenly a swarm of guards dressed in all black riot gear descended on the group.

Rock could see his devotees starting to give way a little, however all they needed was one more small push before they could break out into a full-on riot, and he knew just how to provide that push.

He made his way through the crowd and punched the first guard he saw as hard as he could. Rock leveled the guard with one hard punch to his jaw, sending him crashing to the ground. "THAT WAS FOR THAT OLD MAN YOU'LL BEAT UP IN FRONT OF THE CHOW HALL!"

It wasn't until the other guards started jumping on Rock that his group found the courage to jump in. The group rushed the guards, pulled them off of him, then started beating them mercilessly. The guards didn't stand a chance. They were nowhere near prepared for a full-scale attack.

After the guards were fully subdued, the rioting convicts looked around in a confused state. They had no idea what to do next, until their fearless leader Rock led the charge for the gate.

"BLACK POWER!" he yelled as he prompted his group to shake the gate until it gave way.

"NOW LET'S TEAR THIS MA FUCKA APART!" Rock said while carefully observing his surroundings. He looked up and saw that the guy in the gun tower finally stepped out. He was equipped with a fully loaded thirty thirty in his white sweaty hands.

He could see him yelling something. However, he couldn't make out what he was saying due to the loud roars of the out-of-control crowd. At this point the entire prison population was in pandemonium.

While other prisoners were fulfilling their jail house fantasy, getting revenge on guards that had disrespected them, or openly raping female staff members that they always wanted. Rock was headed in the opposite direction towards the gate that separated the jail and the staff parking lot.

Rock pulled out a small piece of paper and followed Ms. Byran's directions to a specific spot in the yard. He kneeled down, digging with his fingers the spot where she said the wire cutters would be. When he failed to find them, he looked at his directions again. However, by this time the guards had called in reinforcements and were starting to take control of the situation. They were starting to shoot people and dispersing tear gas. The tear gas was so thick that Rock found it hard to see or breathe. He ripped off his shirt and rapped it around his head and nose area.

After a couple of bullets ripped through the grass near him, Rock decided to run across the field and back into the institution. "Where the fuck is Kya's people?" he questioned himself.

Things seemed bleak for him; nothing was going as planned for him.

Prior to this, Rock had been running the track for months, training for this very moment. So, it didn't take him long to catch up with the other convicts. He ran through the crowd and was astounded at what he saw. Prisoners were running ramped throughout the whole institution.

Everywhere Rock turned he saw convicts either gang raping a female staff member, stabbing each other, or sodomizing one of the guards.

He felt some sorrow for one of them. The cool guard that he used to start this riot. However, when he attempted to grab his coat as he ran by, Rock slapped him hard across his face, and kept it pushing. No matter how cool a dude was, he was far from worth his freedom. *Fuck that devil*, he thought to himself as he made it past the chow hall and headed towards the control area. He knew that once he made it past this area, he was home free.

The only question now was how he was going to make it through the metal door. He ran up to it and pulled the handle as hard as he could. It didn't budge. He then put his face up to the glass and attempted to peer through it. He could only see shadowy male figures through the two-way mirror.

At this point, Rock was frustrated and confused. Where was the Jamaican calvary that Kya had promised him? The calvary that he paid a quarter of a million dollars to obtain?

He began to have doubts about the whole situation. Maybe something went wrong on the block and Reek wasn't able to get up the money for his small army? Or maybe Kya stiffed him? Rock quickly dismissed that idea, knowing that Kya would never give up the opportunity to bust him out of jail.

Becoming the new Don gave Kya a lot of responsibilities, yet he still had a lot to prove, and busting Rock out of State Prison in broad daylight would make a good impression on those who were watching him, foreign and domestic.

Rock could hear loud voices coming from inside the control room. He placed his ear against the mirrored glass, and almost got his head blown off in the process. A bullet crashed through the window, shattering it to pieces. Rock ducked for cover just in time as large shards of glass rained on him like R. Kelly did that young girl in that sex tape.

He didn't know whether the bullet came from inside the control center or from the gun tower. What he did know was he wasn't about to blow an opportunity to escape out the open window.

Rock took in two quick breaths and keeping his head low ran opposite the door, stopped, then turned around in a crouched posture like an Olympic sprinter. Suddenly, he took off as fast as he could towards the door. His plan was to do a jumping dive through the shattered window.

At the last moment just before he could perform his acrobatic feat, Rock hard the door pop open and in order to avoid a collision had to stop short. Inches from his freedom, he put his hands up in a boxer's position, intent on knocking the first person who came out the door clean out.

For him it was all or nothing. Freedom or death. He came too far to turn back.

When a face finally appeared in the doorway, he jabbed at it with all he had, but only connected with the edge of the door when the person saw it coming and closed the door seconds before impact.

"AGHHHHHH SHIT!" Rock screamed, clutching his hand in pain.

"COM YEEEW IREE?" a masked man questioned in a deep Jamaican accent.

Rock's pain instantly subsided once he realized his rescue squad had finally arrived.

They entered the control room and was met by a heavily armed group of five soldiers, dressed in all black from head to toe. They shoved a pistol into his hand, then escorted him out of the building like he was the President. Rock smiled as he headed towards the door that separated him from his freedom. However, when he got outside his celebration was short-lived.

The prison parking lot was surrounded by uniformed sheriffs. Most of them were kneeling by their cruisers, while others stood with their guns drawn in a firing position. The whole scene reminded Rock of a bad episode of the Wire.

The hired Jamaican mercenaries lived up to their name. As soon as they assessed the situation, they spread out and began to fire on the cops. Semi-automatic shells ripped through the cruisers with breakneck force, as the officers ran and ducked for cover.

Rock also ran for cover when the cops started to return fire.

Men on both sides were dropping like flies.

Rock ran to the side of the building, aimed, then fired, "BOCK, BOCK, BOCK, CLICK!" His gun was finally out of ammunition.

He looked to see how much of his team was still left and noticed that most of them were either dead or mortally wounded.

Rock hated to leave them, but he had no choice. Either he left now or joined them in the afterlife. Besides, he reasoned if he didn't make it then, their deaths would have been in vain.

He sneakily made his way across the side of the wall, then ventured out onto the road.

"ONE OF THEM'S GETTING AWAY!" he heard somebody yell behind him. Rock ignored him and just kept on running.

He was out of breath and at least a football's field away from the prison when he felt a sharp pain sting him on the side of his stomach. He looked down to find the entire bottom half of his shirt and pants soaked with blood.

He attempted to continue running, however his legs had long since abandoned him.

Out of breath he collapsed on the side of the road. Rock was losing blood quickly and fighting to maintain consciousness. He teetered between unconsciousness and consciousness. He could hear but couldn't see what was going on around him.

Suddenly, he felt something or somebody tugging on him.

He hard the sound of a car door slamming, followed by a female voice. *Damn he was caught*, he thought to himself. He came so close to escaping.

He heard the sounds of a big explosion in the distance. No doubt the last of his Jamaican crew giving them crackers hell with a grenade.

Rock fought to open his eyes. His vison was blurry, so he blinked them continuously in an attempt to see better. The blinking didn't help much, however before blacking out he was able to steal a glimpse of the woman driving the car. She was a petite white girl with gray eyes and long beautiful blond hair.

A Sneak Peek at
"Crack City"

Chapter 1

R ock woke up, or so he thought, face to face with himself. He was suspended approximately ten feet over his own body.

He thought to himself, *them crackers then finally got me.* All the dirt of robbing, killing, hustling, fornicating and treachery had finally caught up with him.

He stilled his thoughts to listen to the preacher. His funeral was about to begin. "Dearly beloved," the tall, dark-skinned, gray-haired man dressed in all black said. "We are gathered here today to lay to rest a good man. Another brother slain and cut down before his time."

"AMEN!" somebody yelled from the audience.

"He was known on this earthly plain as brother Duane Maleek Robarts, but in the kingdom of heaven he will be known as an angel. JESUS will now take you into his bosom and carry him on to salvation."

At the moment the preacher mentioned Jesus, Rock became so upset that one could have literally fried an egg on his forehead, had he had one. He was madder than a Nazi at a Black Panther Party meeting. It wasn't that he had something against Jesus Christ, because he actually revered the man as a prophet of course, but not as a God.

Rock was born a Muslim, and his crackhead mother Stacy knew that, so why did she disrespect his corpse by giving him a fucken Christian burial.

He cursed her, then changed his mind once he looked into her tear-stained face and eyes. She was only doing what she felt was best for her only son.

He looked at the woman with her arms wrapped firmly around his mother. He couldn't believe his ghostly eyes. What the fuck was that trifling bitch doing here? Attempting to console Rock's mother was none other than his treacherous ex-girlfriend, Rena.

"If anybody would like to pay their last respects you may do so at this time," the preacher said, concluding his eulogy.

Rena, Rock's mother and Rena's two-year-old son by his rat ass cousin, all walked up to his mahogany covered casket holding hand. His mother was distraught. She was really taking his death hard. It seemed like the closer she got to his lifeless body, the more emotional she became.

Rena was also crying. However, Rock knew that they could only be crocodile tears, because cold-blooded creatures like her ate their own young.

"AUUGGGG!" Suddenly Stacy broke free from Rena's grip, and lunged hands first towards his casket, nearly toppling it over in the process. She reached into the coffin and began to beat him savagely about his chest and arms. As other family members attempted to restrain her, she began to shake him violently.

"WAKE UP BABY . . . YOU ARE NOT DEAD!" she yelled repeatedly into his ear.

He was so transfixed by what was going on that he could actually feel himself being pounced on. Suddenly everything went black. *This was it*, he thought, *I'm finally going to the hell fire.*

For some odd reason he felt himself starting to get aroused. His dick seemed to have a mind of its own. Even in death it worked. He tried to ignore it; he had bigger things to worry about, like negotiating with the prince of hell for his soul, however the feeling was too strong.

He heard the sounds of a female voice saying, "You not dead big boy, take . . . ta . . . take this white pussy."

Cindy was having the time of her life, raping Rock as she'd done for the past three years. Every chance she got to be alone with him, she would slip out of her bra and panties, suck his dick to life, then straddle him sliding her hot wet pussy down the length of his pole.

Just last week she almost got caught when Lanceen came home early from one of her many errands. However, this time she had him all to herself. Lanceen had to go on a thirty-day training exercise with the F.B.I. However, she made sure that before she left she'd given her strict instructions to make sure to keep his feeding tube clean and filled, to bathe him daily and to make sure to rotate his limp body so he wouldn't contract any bed sores. And Cindy made sure to rotate him thoroughly every hour on the hour.

No sooner than Lanceen was out the door, Cindy had fixed the comatose Rock and herself an intimate candlelit dinner. She dimmed the lights and ate next to his bed.

The atmosphere she set was cozy and romantic, and she found herself talking to the unconscious man, as she often did, confessing to him her most intimate and darkest secrets.

After dinner, Cindy started her freaky sexual escapades. First taking his feeding tube out and replacing it with her tongue, then peeling the covers back and relieving him of every stich of clothing. To her delight and surprise his dick was already hard. She decided to suck on it anyway. *After all,* she thought, *practice made perfect.* Besides, she was planning on raping him all night, and she knew that if she could make him cum through oral pleasure, the next nut would take him a lot longer to bust.

She hog spit a large warm slimy glob of flehm onto the head of his cock. Then watched intently as it descended down the length of his thick penis. She was waiting for the spit to reach midway, so she could chase it down with her warm mouth and catch it. Finally, the moment had arrived.

She licked her think pink lips in anticipation, then opened her mouth wide and caught the spit before it reached his balls.

She stripped out of her clothing while vigorously sucking on his cock, playing with his balls, and inserting two fingers into her own hot juicy pussy, all at the same time. Up and down, side to side, was the motion that caused Rock to ejaculate deeply into her throat. His penis jerked and pulsated as she gingerly swallowed his essence, then continued to suck his dick back to stiffness.

Cindy roughly jerked him off while using her other hand to reach into the bedstand drawer and retrieve a condom. She rolled the latex over the length of his cock, then stared at it, transfixed on how massive a black man's penis actually was. Now she realized why her racist father had warned her so sternly not to get caught dead with a black man. *But how could something so pleasurable be bad*, she thought to herself, as she sneakily looked both ways over her shoulders as if she was a cat burglar about to steal the Crown Jewels.

She returned her gaze to daddy's stern warning, then rolled the condom off and threw it on the floor. "For once in my life I want to see what you really feel like inside of me big boy."

Rock smirked as if he heard her freaky comment.

The sudden gesture startled her, causing her to stumble backwards off the bed, and hit her head on the back wall. She grabbed the back of her head in pain, using the wall and her legs to help herself back to her feet.

"Naw . . . he can't be," she whispered to herself, as she turned the lights on, and began to slowly walk toward the bed.

She looked into his motionless face, then shook him. No reaction. She yelled at him, "ARE YOU AWAKE BABY?" Still no reaction.

Cindy observed his naked form from head to toe, and noticed his stomach was bigger, no doubt from a lack of exercise. She also took note that his bullet wound was almost completely gone.

She looked at his limp penis laying his leg like a dead garden snake. She smiled, then returned her gaze back to his face.

"If you don't want me to suck your cock again, please speak now or forever hold your peace."

She straddled Rock's face with her pussy, then bent over sixty-nine style and gently put his limp penis back into her mouth. Her long blond hair tickled his legs and balls as her head went up and down to the rhythm of her own inner drum. She moaned as his penis sprung back to life in her wet, warm oral cavity. Cindy turned around and started kissing him as she massaged his tool and rubbed the head of it up and down the sweet opening of her pink slippery pussy lips.

Slowly inserting his penis into her hot wet love nest, she threw her head back and gasped for air.

"Wake up baby, you are not dead . . . taka . . . take this white pussy," she moaned as she took his whole dick into her tight hot white pussy.

Suddenly, Rock found himself clawing his way headfirst out of a deep dark tunnel. He was then greeted by the brightest light he'd ever seen in his entire life.

Somebody grabbed him and pulled him out, probing his nose and mouth with what looked like a blue rubber tube. His heart was beating rapidly. The whole scene reminded him of an alien abduction gone bad. *Damn, death was hard*, Rock thought to himself.

When was he going to get to the part where he would hustle the devil for his eternal soul back? He could hear a baby crying in the distance. Wait a minute was that him? He listened closely and realized that was him. He was the baby crying, but how?

All of a sudden reality set in. He was back in Newark, New Jersey's Beth Israel Hospital, being born again. He felt overjoyed when somebody passed him to his mother. Rock looked her in her fresh face and realized for the first time how beautiful she actually was. She looked so flawless and young before drugs and the streets had stolen her beauty, health and youth.

He felt so comfortable and loved wrapped up in her protective, warm embrace. *Maybe I'm not dead*, he thought. *Maybe this is what the Christians really meant when they said you will die in this world, then be born again in Christ.*

He now hugged his mother tightly, and secretly thanked her for the Christian burial. Just as he began to make plans for the future, he blacked out once again.

When he awakened next, he was at the moment in his life when he found his very first package. *I guess it's true what they say about your whole life flashing before your eyes when you die. Maybe, this was God's cruel way of showing people their mistakes before he punished them*, Rock thought to himself.

Reek was eleven, and Rock thirteen when they first met in their native Haze Homes projects. They had both been walking around aimlessly, searching for some food. By chance, they locked eyes on each other from across the parking lot.

It had been a record breaking 48 inches of snow that fell that morning and both him and Reek were outside with little more than thin ripped up leather jackets and holey corduroy jeans. They looked like the garbage can kids.

Both of their mothers shared crack addictions. Both have been in the habit of selling themselves to support their addictions. Everything went towards crack; welfare checks they received for their sons. Government issued cheese was even sold for crack. Truth be told, had it not been for the fact that Section 8 pays for their Public Housing or that too would have been up for sale.

Rock was cold, hungry and frustrated at the fact that he had to spend his childhood with the responsibilities of an adult. Rock stalked over to Reek in his tattered Pro-wing sneakers, "WHAT THE YOU LOKKIN AT?" he said, towering over the smaller, shorter Reek.

"YOU MA FUCKA!" Reek yelled, while poking his chest out, trying and failing to appear bigger.

"Don's make me cold cock you lil nigga," Rock said as he put his hands up and got into his fighting stance; the only thing his pops had taught him before he died.

Reek mimicked Rock's movements, putting his hands up and rocked awkwardly from side to side.

"What you going to fight or dance?" Rock asked him as he busted out in uncontrollable laughter.

"You a tough lil ma fucka . . . what's your name homey?"

"REEK!" he said, still rocking awkwardly from side to side with his hands up protecting his face.

"Come on Reek, you can chill with me," Rock said as he reached in and put his arm around Reek's shoulders, ignoring his funny fighting stance.

"First thing we have to do is teach you how to box," Rock said, then added as an afterthought, "By the way, my name is Rock."

The two young boys got acquainted with each other throughout the day. As the light turned black, the two boys witnessed as they did every night, sights and sounds of the ghetto.

There was an old, ragged dope fiend woman giving a blow job to a local hustler's pit bull in one of the dark corners inside the project building.

The dog was panting and wagging its tail, as he laid on his back, being cheered on by a small group of hustlers and neighborhood fiends alike.

This was a nightly ritual for some of the more hardened criminals in the projects. Their cold moral-less hearts caused them to degrade female fiends in a way unbeknownst to humanity.

To them, fiends were nothing more than soul-less, mindless zombies.

Rock and Reek walked to the edge of their project building, trying to catch a better look at the shootout that was developing right before their very eyes.

"LOOK ROCK!" Reek screamed with excitement, as he pointed towards the action. A cop car was only a half of a block away from a black 5.0 Mustang.

As the Mustang rounded the corner, the passenger peeked half of his body out of the sun roof, shooting at the pursuing squad car with a Uzi machine gun.

This is a scene right out of a movie, Rock thought to himself as he watched the driver round the corner and throw something out of the window, then sped away up the block, creating even more distance between them and their pursuers.

"COME ON REEK!" Rock whispered, urging his new friend to follow him. "I THINK THEM NIGGA'S JUST TOSSED A BAG OF FOOD OUT THE WINDOW!" Rock said with excitement.

Reek's little eyes lit up at the thought of eating something. The two boys hadn't eaten at all that day. Rock and Reek cautiously approached the black bag. Their stomachs growled audibly, scaring off a cat that was also persistently pursuing its meal for the night.

Rock knelt down and unzipped the black duffle bag that was laying in the snow. "What is it?" Reek questioned impatiently. "Is it some food?"

"I don't know," Rock responded, not knowing what to make of the white powdered substance. "It looks like some type of flour or snow," Rock continued.

Hunger overpowered logic and in a rush to get some food into his stomach, Reek had pushed Rock out of the way, tripping over his own feet, falling headfirst into the bag.

"What is it?" Rock questioned, as Reek picked himself up and attempted, unsuccessfully to brush the white substance out of his hair and face. "I feel weird," Reek said after several minutes. Rock looked at his boy intently. His eyes were opened very wide, and he began to shake. "What's wrong with you?"

"I don't know. My face feels all funny," Reek said as he sat down on the curb, unable to maintain his balance.

"Yo Reek, you look like my moms when she be getting high off that stuff."

"I feel real lightheaded," Reek responded, getting up, then falling back over in the snow, with a wide goofy grin on his face.

Rock walked over to the duffle bag and began to inspect its contents. He licked his fingertips, dipped them into the bag, then tested the powder. As he had seen other hustlers do before him, he opened his mouth widely and took in a deep breath. He knew that if his tongue became numb, it was cocaine in the bag.

"Reek are you sure you aiight?" he asked while standing him back up and examining him.

"Yeah, I'm aiight," Reek said, still suffering from the ill effects of the cocaine.

Rock grabbed him by his shoulders and guided him into the hallway of their building, while keeping the bag tucked tightly between themselves.

Once safely inside, he sat him down on the staircase. Rock looked around cautiously, making sure they were alone. Even though people rarely visited the top floor, at times fiends would come up there to shoot up, or a hustler would come up there to get their dick sucked by a female who came short or didn't have any money at all. A fiend would exchange a blow job for some drugs. That's how the ghetto worked; we functioned off of the barter system.

Rock sat next to his new friend and placed the bag between them.

"Are you sure you aiight?"

"I think I'm cool now that we out of the cold." Reek rubbed his hand together and blew into them for warmth; a thick cloud of smoke appeared.

"Now what's in the bag?"

Rock opened the bag and they both peered in. "I... I think it's coke."

"Oh shit, coke," Reek responded, while looking around cautiously. "What we gone do with that?"

"Sale it... what you think?" Rock responded with a 'come on are you serious,' look on his face.

"We can't sale no coke."

"And why not?" Rock asked.

"We too young, and somebody might try and take it from us," Reek said with a paranoid look on his face.

Rock knew he had a valid point, but just didn't care. "Well, that's a chance we gone have to take," Rock bravely said, then continued, "You hungry ain't you?"

Reek put his head down and regarded his howling stomach. He couldn't deny the fact that he was extremely hungry. Like Rock he hadn't eaten in almost two days.

"So how we gone sale it without getting robbed?" asked Reek.

Rock put his head down in deep thought.

Several minutes later he picked his head back up with excitement in his eyes. "Who's the biggest Haze Homes hustler around here?" Rock asked.

"AKBAR!" they both yelled in unison.

"So, why don't we just say we running for him?" Rock asked, paused, then continued, "as long as we stay on the down low we should be aiight."

"Quick, help me pick up some of these empties."

Reek and Rock scrambled on the floor and picked up as many empty coke bottles as they could. The floor was littered with them—bottles of all shapes, sizes and colors. In the dim light the floor looked like a dirty bag of Skittles.

Early the next morning Reek and Rock was on the block selling their colorful bottles of coke. To their surprise they were the first ones out there, and why that be, it was 5:15 a.m.

Akbar had his men working on shifts of three's, morning, evening, and night. He ran his business like a twenty-four hour 7-Eleven, except there they didn't sale soda pops and hot dogs. They sold everything from cocaine, crack, heroin, pills and weed. However, like any other hood entrepreneurship slash ghetto enterprises, good help was harder to find than Superhead's panties at a JA-RULE video shoot.

And since his righthand man and Captain of the Haze Homes Hustlers was always late with his drug deliveries, shop didn't usually open until around 8:00 a.m. So that gave Rock and Reek almost three hours of free reign on the block.

Rock was thorough and organized. He would screen the customers while Reek served them. And whenever Reet ran out of product, Rock would be the one to replenish the stash.

Their first drug transaction was the hardest. Rock was posted up on the corner of the block while Reek stayed hidden close to the building. They both watched as the same tattered sedan cruised up and down the street, obviously looking for somebody or something.

Finally the car stopped in the middle of the street. The man driving rolled down his dingy windows and waved Rock over. He was nervous, but still wanted to appear hard, so he ran over to the car with a mean mug planted firmly on his young face.

"YO!" the skinny gray looking man started off. "You seen Raheem out here?" he asked, while randomly scratching himself about his head, neck, and crotch region.

"Naw . . . why what's up?" Rock countered with his little chest poked out.

The man looked at him suspect, then observed the streets for police activity. "How about Akbar, you seen him?"

Once the notorious name of Akbar was mentioned, Rock knew exactly what the man was looking for, crack.

"Akbar not around right now, but his work is," Rock said while leaning arrogantly against the car.

The man looked at him again suspiciously. he didn't trust the tall, dirty looking teenager, but he was fiending for his morning fix. And on top of all that, he was going to be late for work if he didn't get on the road soon. "Okay what you got youngin?"

"What you want?" Rock countered.

"Two dimes."

Rock turned towards Reek and put up two fingers, then made a fist, which told Reek to bring two dimes.

He then turned his attention back to the driver, who was now thinking about jacking the two young boys for their product.

Rock bravely reached his hand into the car window, "You know how Akbar do it fam, no play before pay."

The man reluctantly reached into his pockets and pulled out two crumbled up ten-dollar bills and handed it over to him.

Any thoughts the driver had of taking off with the young boy's drugs abandoned him with the mere mention of the ruthless kingpin's name.

The rest of the morning went smoothly. Rock and Reek got rid of a half an ounce before Akbar's men came on the scene and commandeered the block.

It was now 8:00 a.m. and they were due for school.

Since they both had been so bad at their former school, Spencer, the school district had no other alternative but to send them to 13th Avenue school. They both hated that place with a passion.

Before the invasion of the Bloods and Crips, whole sections of Brick City was at war with each other. And 13th Avenue was considered hostile and enemy territory for them.

Every day after school the 13th Avenue kids would chase them as far as South Orange Avenue and Burgan Street, almost seven blocks away.

"All maaan, we going be late as hell . . . and Ms. Haywood said she gone beat my ass with a ruler if I came late again," Reek said.

"Damn Reek, you scary as hell," Rock teased.

"Let's take a shortcut," Reek suggested.

They both started walking in the direction of their school, then Rock stopped short.

"Come on man we gotta hurry if we gone make it to breakfast."

"Wait a minute Reek. How much money we got?" Rock asked, remembering about the money they just made.

"I don't know." Reek dug into his pockets and pulled out a wad of tens, fives and twenties, then handed it to him. "Here, you count it."

At the time Rock wasn't the best reader, but he was a whiz at math. In fact math was the only subject in school he was actually passing.

Rock looked around cautiously, then stuffed the money into his pockets as fast as he could. By that time West Kinney High was filled with students smoking everything from cigarettes to weed blunts in front of the building.

A lone security guard rushed out and asked, "WHY YOU KIDS OUT HERE SMOKING AND JOKING AND NOT IN SCHOOL YET?"

"GET YO DUMB ASS OUTTA HERE," one of the kids in the crowed responded, then chucked an empty Old English 800 beer can at him, hitting the older man on top of his head.

"WHO . . . WHO THREW THAT?" the guard yelled while retreating into the safety of the school building, barely escaping a ST.IDES 40-ounce bottle.

The crowd exploded with laugher, then went back to their morning ritual of smoking and drinking.

Luckily for Rock and Reek the high school kids were too busy with their entertainment to focus on them, and the nine hundred dollars that Rock just stuffed in his pockets.

"Damn Reek, why you give me the dough out here?"

"Oh . . . my bag." Reek put his head down, just now realizing his mistake. "I thought you wanted it."

"Next time we'll do it in the building aiight?"

Reek shook his head in agreement.

"It's okay homeboy. You gone get it." Rock put a comforting hand around his friend's shoulder. "But right now let's catch this five Kinney bus so we won't miss breakfast."

Reek and Rock jumped on the bus excited that they would make it to school in time to catch breakfast. For the most part, breakfast and lunch was the only reason they had even attended school in the first place. It was only at the weekends that they had to worry about food, because school wasn't open then, and relying on their crackhead parents was just out of the question.

The bus stopped and a group of teenage girls boarded, snickered at them, then sat down across from each other. Rock put his head down and looked at his dirty jeans, sneakers and coat, then viewed an equally bummed out Reek.

"I'm tired of this shit," Rock said.

"What?" Reek responded.

Just then one of the teenage girls turned around in her seat and said to him, "Excuse me, but me and my girlfriends want to know which one of these garbage cans you live in?" The comment caused the crowd of girls to go crazy with laughter.

Rock turned towards Reek, "That shit right their. You know what," he continued, "after school we gone get fresh."

Reek nodded his head in agreement.

Later on that day, after school, Rock and Reek found themselves once again running for their lives. A group of five teenagers were chasing them up the street. After about ten minutes of running from the boys and the rocks and bottles they violently hurled at them, the boys had finally given up. Rock and Reek kneeled near a McDonald's restaurant catching their breaths.

"REEK I'M GETTING TIRED OF THIS RUNNING SHIT!" Rock yelled between breaths.

"ME TOO!" Reek responded equally out of breath.

"I SWARE ONE OF THESE DAYS I'M GOING KILL ONE OF THOSE 13TH AVENUE NIGGAS."

"I hear you Reek," Rock retorted, finally catching his breath.

"Now let's go get fresh." Rock put an arm around Reek and led him into a sneaker store. The boys walked into the footwear establishment looking at the sneaker racks with amazement. It wasn't that they'd never been there before, because they had. However, this had been the first time they actually had enough money to purchase anything.

They were immediately spotted by the Sales Manager. Because of their dirty appearance and skin color, the white Manager had made a conscious decision to keep a close eye on them.

A young thick Puerto Rican girl was the first one person brave enough to approach them. Though the girl named Maria was only sixteen, she was overdeveloped for her age. With two double D breasts, thick, full athletic legs and long curly black hair, she looked like she could be closely related to Vanessa Del Rio.

As she approached, Rock couldn't keep his eyes off this short thick Latin beauty. With every step she bounced causing her soft luscious breasts to jiggle.

"Hello, welcome to V.I.M. My name is Maria. Can I help you?" she said with a professional smile.

Rock and Reek couldn't believe that the girl didn't treat them or look at them indifferently because of their dirty appearance. Either this girl was blind or totally oblivious to the fact that Reek and Rock were not wearing the latest of fashions, to say the least.

Much to his surprise she grabbed Rock by the hand and led him into the store. Reek followed closely behind them, focused on the girl's bouncy ass.

"What sizes is y'all?" she asked while pushing them into a row of seats. When Rock tried to protest she put a manicured hand up and said, "Trust me. I know what'll look good on you."

"I'm a size ten."

"And I'm a size eight and a half," Reek added.

When the girl bounced away Reek tapped him on his shoulder, "Yo, I think she digging you."

"Me too," Rock agreed. They both grinned at each other and privately cracked jokes on people until Maria returned with several pairs of sneakers and boots. She laid the boxes before their feet. When she kneeled and reach for Rock's old dirty Pro Wings, he withdrew his feet with embarrassment. he didn't know what embarrassed him more, his dirty sneakers or even dirtier socks.

She grabbed him gently by the hand and they locked eyes for the first time, "I understand." She got up and left. When she returned she handed him two fresh pairs of socks.

"Here, put these on first." She tossed them the socks, then turned around so as not to embarrass them further.

Reek and Rock quickly stripped out of their sneakers and socks and put the new socks on.

"Reek toss these in the trash," Rock whispered while handing him his shoes and socks.

Maria turned around and placed a fresh pair of High Tech boots on his feet. "Those look good on you."

"You think so?" Rock questioned while standing and checking them out in the store's full length wall mirror.

"I know so," Maria responded, seductively licking her luscious lips.

"Then I'll take it. Reek you good?" he asked while turning towards his friend.

Reek had on a pair of brand new black and white low top British Knights. Reek put a wide smile on his face and Rock had his answer. They walked to the register with their new footwear. Maria rang them up while the manager stood behind them with his arms folded, as if expecting them to make a run for it at any moment.

Rock pulled out a wad of money, glimpsed at the manager who now had an open look of shock on his pale face, then paid for the items. When Maria handed him the change and receipt, he discovered that she scribbled her name and number on the back of it.

"Thank you for shopping at V.I.M.," she said when they had turned to walk away.

"Thank you," Rock responded, turning around and finding Maria giving him the signal to call her, by placing her thumb to her ear and her pinky finger to her mouth like a phone receiver.

Once outside Reek said, "DAMN BRA THAT GIRL WAS REALLY ON YOU."

"Yeah I'll say. She gave me the digits and all that."

"STOP LIMING," Reek said, trying to wrestle the piece of paper out of Rock's hands. He swung the paper in the air while Reek jumped up and down trying to retrieve it. After about five minutes he finally let him see it. Reek looked at the girl's number briefly, then gave it back to him.

"So what we going do now?"

"We gone to the arcade."

"I'LL RACE YOU!" Reek took off running towards Broad and Market street, leaving a bunch of angry patrons in his wake, as he darted around some of them and pushed through others. They spent the remainder of the day playing video games until the sun went down.

Chapter 2

"PLEASE AKBAR, PLEEEASE DON'T KILL ME . . . PAH PLEASE . . . AKBAR," Popsickle yelled, while hanging headfirst down the entrance of the incinerator shaft. Akbar's men held him by his feet on the fifteenth floor of one of the Haze Holmes project buildings.

"OH NOW IT'S PLEASE AKBAR PLEASE, WHEN JUST A MINUTE AGO YOU WAS TALKING THAT PRINCE STREET KILLER SHIT," Akbar said between puffs of his chocolate-filled weed blunt.

Akbar was a medium belt brown-skinned old head with a low top fade. He was rocking an all black Adidas sweatsuit, a humongous rose gold watch, and a thick gold Gucci link chain with an A.K.47 charm dangling from it.

A lone fiend walked up the stairwell, saw Akbar and five big black dudes that looked like they ate people for breakfast, wisely put his head down and went back the way he'd came, as if he seen nothing.

"PLEASE, AKBAR, I . . . I . . .I GAVE YOU ALL THE MONEY I HAD," Popsickle cried out.

"ALL THE MONEY YOU HAD, ALL THE MONEY YOU HAD?" Akbar repeated angrily. "NIGGA YOU BETTER COME UP WIT THE REST OF MY BREAD!" He was growing more and more impatient by the second.

Two months ago he fronted Popsickle with half a kilo of coke and had only gotten half of his money back. After numerous attempts at trying to locate him, he had finally caught him slipping. Popsickle was found drunk trying to sneak back from the liquor store with a forty-ounce of Crazy Horse malt liquor in his hands.

"I SWEAR TO GOD I'MA GET YOUR MONEY!" Popsickle screamed out, as he felt something big nibble on his ear, climb over his head, then get tangled up in his shirt.

"COME ON AKBAR, IT'S RATS DOWN HERE," he cried in fear.

Akbar lazily took a sip off of the man's forty-ounce beer, then spit it out and looked at the label. "WHAT THE FUCK YOU GOT ME DRINKING, SOME CHEAP ASS CRAZY HORSE," Akbar said while watching his goons turn towards him and laugh. "I SHOULD KILL YO ASS FOR THIS CHEAP ASS DRINK YOU GOT ME SIPPING." Akbar laughed, got serious again, then continued, "AS A MATTER FACT DROP THAT NIGGA."

His goons looked at each other, shrugged their shoulders, then let the man go. Akbar pushed between the men, put his ear to the entrance of the incinerator and listened intently to Popsickle's head bounce off the sides of the small interior of the incinerator. He listened intently as Popsickle's screams grew faint as he descended violently down the shaft. Suddenly he heard a loud thud. No doubt Popsickle's neck and back breaking, followed by an eerie silence.

The mob of Haze Holmes' hustlers all looked up at each other, busted out in a hysterical laughter, then casually walked down the steps.

Thirty minutes later, Akbar was in his apartment in Little City, getting his dick sucked by an underaged crackhead, while reclining on his La-Z-Boy and watching the Redskins beat the hell out of the Giants on TV. He was barely able to follow the game due to a fifteen-year old Holly, a slim red bone girl from Eat Orange giving him the best head he'd ever had in his life. He felt bad about fucking with this particular teenager, because she just so happen to be his Captain Richie's little sister. However, head was head.

At the ripe old age of forty, Akbar was old enough to be this girl's father, but he didn't care. He reasoned that if he wasn't the one fucking her somebody else would, and why should he deny himself the pleasure of this young girl's tender mouth just because she was his friend's little sister.

His eyes rolled to the back of his head, his toes curled up in his Gore Tech boots, and his body trembled with excitement as he released a white sticky substance into young Holly's little tight mouth.

She swallowed his kids, licked her lips seductively, then put her hand out.

Akbar reach into his pants pocket and pulled out two dime bottles of crack cocaine and handed it over to her. Holly ran to a dark corner of the living room, pulled a glass pipe out of her back pocket, put the crack in the pipe, lit it and took a long deep pull.

Abkar zipped up his jeans and watched her with disgust. "HOLLY DIDN'T I TELL YO DUMB ASS NOT TO BE SMOKING THAT SHIT IN MY PRESENCE?" he yelled.

Holly ignored him and continued to smoke.

He stalked over to her, then snatched her by her long reddish hair. "BITCH, DON'T YOU HEAR ME TALKING TO YOU?"

Her heart began to beat overtime in her chest. Sure Akbar had gotten mad at her before for smoking in front of him, however he'd never had the nerve to put his hands on her before.

Holly didn't know what to do. Should she fight him back, run or plead with him? Apparently Holly didn't make up her mind fast enough, because Akbar began to smack her so hard across the face that her ears began to ring. She literally thought for a moment that she had lost her hearing. She could see his lips moving, but no sound came out. Suddenly her hearing returned to her, and not a moment too soon. She was about to hear the most important message Akbar had ever told her.

"BITCH, IF YOU EVER SMOKE THAT SHIT 'ROUND ME AGAIN, I'M GOING TO MURDER YOU," Akbar said towering over her.

He then rubbed his dick. It was throbbing and hard as a BRINK'S ARMORED TRUCK.

Akbar was a womanizer and a control freak. The fear in the young girl's eyes and the tears that stained her pretty red bone face turned him on.

He snatched her by her hair again, only this time harder.

When Holly tried to crawl away, Akbar snatched her by the back of her jeans, almost ripping them completely off. He lost his grip when Holly tripped and landed face first onto the carpet, jeans wrapped around her ankles.

Holly lay there on the floor with her silk red panties hanging half on, half off her, partially exposing her soft round young ass.

Akbar reached down and tore the rest of her panties away, then attempted to enter her dry, tight pussy from behind. When he realized she wasn't wet, he kissed her about her neck and shoulders attempting to get her aroused.

"NOOO, AKBAR PLEASE . . . I'M, I'M NOT READY," Holly screamed while struggling against his brute strength.

He ignored her pleas and tried to enter her again. When that failed he spit on the head of his dick, then rammed it into her with so much force that Holly felt her heart hit the back of her throat.

"PLEA . . . PLA . . . PLEASE DON'T I . . . I'M A VIRGIN!"

The virgin comment only made him pump harder. After only twelve strokes of Holly's young virgin pussy, Akbar came in her faster than Dale Earnhardt at a Nas Car race.

It wasn't until he'd looked down and saw his penis covered in blood, that he finally realized that Holly was telling the truth.

When he tried to kiss her on her forehead, she cringed in fear, so he decided to go and take a nice hot shower. Alone in washing the evidence of his crime away, so he thought, Akbar was confronted with his own conscious.

Why had he raped his friend Richie's only sister, he asked himself. *She had it coming*, a voice responded in his head. *You was only teaching her a lesson. I bet she'll think twice before smoking crack in your presence again*, the voice continued.

What if she rats me out, he questioned himself. When he got no response, he continued on with his business of washing away what he thought was the only evidence of his crime.

Meanwhile, in the next room, Holly was confused and crying hysterically. She didn't know what to do. She ran to the kitchen and grabbed a long butcher's knife, did a stabbing motion with it in her hands, then put it back down, dismissing the idea, knowing Akbar would have just shot her.

Her body trembled in fear. Holly's palms were also drenched with sweat. She wiped them on her now bloody jeans.

Oh God how she wished she could take a shower and attempt to wash away the past twenty-four hours. His dirty scent was still on her.

She rushed back to the living room. Pain struck her vaginal region with each step. She looked around confused, and undecided on her next move. Suddenly she looked down and saw her trusty crack pipe. It still had the same rock in it from earlier. She reached for it, put it to her lips, then pulled it back, remembering Akbar's rule with fear.

Fuck Akbar's rule, she thought to herself, suddenly feeling herself brave.

Holly sat down on the floor and started smoking, still in disbelief that Akbar had raped her and taken the most precious thing she had left, her virginity.

* * * * *

Meanwhile, Akbar's Captain and Holly's big brother Richie, was combing the streets as they did every night, looking for his crackhead runaway of a sister. However, it was something about this night that had him more worried about her than ever before.

Ever since a freak fire claimed the lives of both their parents, Holly's been on a self-destructive rampage. Experimenting with all types of drugs, and probably ducking, sucking, and fucking every Tom, Dick and Harry from Newark to Canada, for all he knew.

Holly blamed herself for the fire, even though it wasn't really her fault. On the night in question, her parents were sound asleep, and twelve-year old Holly had gotten a hold of a book of matches. She had decided to go into the living room and play with them. She knew that playing with matches was wrong but didn't understand why. Her father had made the costly mistake of failing to explain it to her. He just snatched them out of her hand whenever he caught her playing with them and gave her a stern look.

However, this time he wasn't around to stop her. She peeked over her slender shoulders, then began to strike match after match, gaze at the fire, then blow it out just before it burned her little fingers.

Once the last match was struck, she gazed at it as before, blew it out, then discarded it onto the carpet.

How could she have known that the last match that she'd thrown would catch the carpet on fire and burn their house down, killing her parents and almost taking herself out in the process. Had it not been for Richie sneaking into the house late, seeing the fire and carrying her to safety, she too would have perished.

But that was three years ago, and his little sister wasn't so little anymore.

He cursed the day she was born when he witnessed his little sister start to develop titties and an ass. She was still petite; however her breast were hand-sized and perky. Her butt wasn't all that big, but the arch that she had, and her curvy hips made up for that.

His dick involuntarily stiffened at the thought of his little sister's curvaceous body. He'd never thought of her in a sexual way and had now felt ashamed that she had actually gotten a reaction out of him.

Suddenly, it began to pour down raining.

Richie felt like he was in the middle of a rain forest. The water felt good to him. Maybe the water would wash away the impure thoughts he just had about his little sister.

He tilted his head back, opened his mouth wide and took in as much water as he could. The cold rain felt good against his skin, however he felt that too much of a good thing was bad, so he ran to his Acura NSX and jumped in.

Before starting the engine and conceding to the search, he remembered a saying that his good friend Akbar had said to him when he first told him about his missing sister. He told him between clouds of a KOOL 100 cigarette smoke, "Richie my friend, you can take the girl out the streets, but you can't take the streets out the girl."

Those words now resonated in his ears like church bells during Sunday Mass and haunting his thoughts like the ghost of Christmas past.

He now considered driving straight to Akbar's house and asking him what he'd meant when he'd said that, however quickly dismissed that idea knowing that Akbar hated surprise unannounced visits.

Still, he had had an uncontrollable urge to just drive to his house.

* * * * *

Meanwhile, Akbar lay awake in his bed with his arms wrapped tightly around Holly's waist and shoulders.

After tonight's earlier altercation, he wasn't taking any chances. Sure he felt kind of bad about roughly taking her virginity, however he didn't feel bad enough to leave himself vulnerable to attack.

Akbar never trusted crackheads, especially a crackhead that's been through as much as Holly had been through.

He thought of all crackheads as soulless, mindless, zombies that would do anything to get a fix, even kill, and he refused to be a victim of the game.

He waited for just the right moment to jump out of the shower, after Holly was good and high out of her mind.

When she'd darted by him and ran into the bathroom, the look in her eyes gave him the impression that she hadn't even registered what had happened to her. However, unbeknownst to him, Holly would never forget what happened to her and she vowed that one day she would get her revenge.

That night in the shower she scrubbed herself over and over again. But no matter how hard or often she washed, the filth from Akbar's rape would not come off. Every time she scrubbed herself clean, she could feel his dirty little hands grabbing and smacking on her ass, and the unwanted intrusion of his hard crooked demon member.

She finally jumped out of the shower and dried herself off with a towel. The rape she'd just endured was so real to her, she still couldn't believe that Akbar had had the audacity to actually rape her.

Holly was so angry that her body trembled uncontrollably. And the crack that she just smoked wasn't helping. Sure it numbed the pain a little, however it ran a muck on her nervous system. Before this she had actually considered abandoning the lethal drug and Akbar's trifling ass, but in light of the most recent events, she might only be able to do without one of them, Akbar, but only after she received just compensation for all her pain and suffering. Beware of a woman scorned. She may be the most dangerous of all foes.

Now she lay there pretending to be asleep, while Akbar held her in his cold dead embrace. The touch from his clammy hands made her skin crawl.

She hated him now; his smell, his face, his everything.

Unable to sleep, Holly tightened her grip on the small steak knife that she secretly held hidden between her knees, and contemplated on whether or not she should cut his dick off while he slept and watch excitedly as he bled out.

Chapter 3

"**W**HERE DID YOU GET THOSE NEW SNEAKERS FROM NIGGA?" Ms. Wills, Reeks crackhead mother asked him, as she swung the homemade extension cord at his almost nude form.

Reek scrambled to the corner of his small bedroom, and balled up, attempting to protect himself. He couldn't believe that just seconds ago he was in his bed sleeping soundlessly, now he was being attacked by his crack crazed mother. He could tell she was fiending for drugs by the wild deer caught in the headlights look in her eyes.

Ms. Willa's skinny form was drenched in sweat as she towered over him with a pair of his new sneakers in one hand and her weapon of choice in the other. She slashed him a couple more times with the extension cord about his head and back, before sitting down on the edge of his bed exhausted, his frail bony chest breathing heavily.

She used her forearm and back of her hands to wipe her face, regaining her composure.

Reek looked at his neglectful piece of shit of a mother and hated the fact that they looked so much alike.

"WHERE'S MY MONEY NIGGA?"

"Wha ... what money Ma?" Reek asked, with a confused look on his young face.

"WHAT MONEY?" she yelled. "THE MONEY YOU USED TO COP THESE NEW SNEAKERS!" She stood up and threw the sneakers at him as evidence.

Reek avoided one sneaker, while the other one smacked him hard on the forehead, then landed awkwardly on his lap.

She began to tear into his room like a fanatical, overzealous D.E.A. agent, opening up his dresser drawers, sifting through them, then slamming them shut.

Ms. Willa locked eyes with her son and noticed that he kept looking at his mattress.

"Ohhh, you hiding my loot in yo mattress?"

When she reached for the mattress Reek finally stood up, then quickly sat back down when Willa picked up her extension cord hand and flinched at him. Reek couldn't handle another slashing no matter how much money was involved.

She flipped over the mattress and found a decent sized pall of tens, fifties and twenties. Her eyes grew wide, her palms began to sweat, and she suddenly had an uncontrollable urge to scratch herself. And scratch herself she did, reaching through the small opening in her dingy boxer briefs, then digging through her thick black pubic hairs with reckless disregard, or care that her son was presently in the same room.

Reek looked at his thieving mother with disgust and contempt in his eyes.

Willa noticed that he was looking at her scratch herself and belligerently asked, "Damn nigga what you want some pussy or somethin'?"

Reek turned his face up at her in disbelief. He couldn't believe the words that just came out of his mother's moraless mouth.

Instead of the look on her son's face making her feel remorseful, it infuriated her, and she decided that it was time that her big time drug dealer of a son learned a lesson. She roughly snatched a hand full of his coarse hair, parted her skinny legs widely in a half-squatted position, then jerked his head into the pit of her salty crotch.

The smell of her vaginal regions was squalidly pungent.

Reek had no other choice but to taste the saltiness of his mother's stash, as she swished and jerked his head back and forth between her legs.

He spit out a couple of her putrid pubic hairs when Willa finally released her death grip on him.

"DON'T TURN YO FACE UP NOW." She paused then continued, "YOU WAS LOOKING AT ME LINE YOU WANTED TO TASTE SOME PLACENTA JUICE!"

When Reek put his head down with shame, her feelings was hurt, so she took her newly found riches and departed.

Just when Reek thought his ordeal was at an end, his drug induced stepfather staggered into the room smelling like a liquor store, then beat him mercilessly for what seemed like hours.

* * * * *

While Reek was being tortured, Rock was in the opposite position. He awakened with Maria, the girl he met at V.I.M., planted firmly in his arms.

He slowly raised his head and peeked over her shoulders. Maria was still sound asleep, or so he thought. He felt his morning wood pulsating underneath the covers and wondered how hard of a sleeper Maria actually was. He decided he'll put it to the test. He dipped his hand under the covers, then softly rubbed on her thick thighs. He wanted to see if she had panties on. She did, so he attempted to slowly ease them off.

Maria stirred in her sleep and Rock stopped.

He thought briefly on how he was going to sex her without her waking up, and had decided to simply pull her thin panties to one side and slide in. His first attempt was unsuccessful. When he tried to penetrate her the elastic from her panties snapped back into place almost chopping his dick off in the process. He tried again, this time striking gold.

Rock knew that he had to be very meticulous in his mining venture. Maria wasn't much of the hard sleeper that he'd earlier hoped for.

He entered her from the side slowly and explored her tight caverns. Using his dick like a shovel, Rock dug deeply into her hot Latin pussy. Her thick pink sugar lips fluttered open, gently wrapped around the head of his tool and engulfed him in warm wetness.

She moaned, then turned around flat on her stomach. Rock matched her motion for motion, being careful not to let cause his rode to slip out of her.

Maria arched her back causing his dick to sink deeper into her pleasurable palace. Rock uncovered their semi-naked bodies and watched as Maria sneakily peeked over her shoulders.

"Oh you was playing possum all that time?" he said.

When she attempted to respond, he rammed the full length of his dick into her, causing her words to come out jumbled and inaudible.

"IDIOS!" she managed to get out before Rock's jouncing became even more intense.

"WHAT . . . WHAT'S THAT?" he tased, while withdrawing his penis ever so slightly, patiently awaiting her response, only to blow her back out whenever she'd opened her mouth.

Maria clinched her lips, refusing to give the black matador the satisfaction of hearing her squeal.

"Oh you think you tough?" Rock said while quoting a character in his favorite movie, *Boys In The Hood*.

He quickly jerked his body, causing Maria's muscles to tense up. She buried her head into her pillow in anticipation of his ramrod.

Rock grew tired of the game and decided to attack the pussy wit a full on assault.

Maria bit down on her pillow and moaned loudly, while shifting her thick hips from side to side. Her breath quickened as she orgasmed a waterfall of pussy juices all over her bed, back and Rock's penis.

He looked down and noticed the sticky white substance plastered all over her Serena Williams like ass. Her soft cakes propelled him with every thrust, causing him to bust his load shortly after. He laid exhausted on his side. Feeling like a Rajah, he demanded that she bring him something to drink.

Maria dressed as fast as she could, wrapping a silk robe around her half nude form and leaving the room, gently closing the door behind her.

Rock folded his hands behind his head, relaxing and staring up to the ceiling. Suddenly the door swung open with so much force that Rock was sure the door handle put a hole through the sheetrock behind it when it slammed into the back wall.

"WHAT THE FUCK?" Rock yelled while sitting up in the bed to see what was going on.

Two men rushed the room, then surrounded both ends of the bed. When he tried to get up they grabbed him by his hands and feet and held him down.

The men were much bigger than himself. However, they still had a little trouble holding the wild struggling teenager down. He swished his head from side to side looking at their Puerto Rican faces, burning their features into his memory for future vengeance.

He thought of screaming for Maria but refused to go out like a bitch. *Besides*, he thought to himself, *she probably the one that set this whole thing up.*

That's when he realized the family resemblance. The two men holding him down were her brothers. Now Rock's suspicions was confirmed. Maria was setting him up, but for what? He didn't have any money, then he remembered the three hundred dollars he had left in his pants pocket laying on the floor.

Suddenly, an older gray-haired version of the two men restraining him appeared in the doorway with a smug Ricky Martin-like look on his face.

"Oh you the little cocksmen that had my little Bambina speaking in tongues last night?"

When Rock tried to respond, Carlos, Maria's father waved a manicured hand up in protest. "No need to explain yourself. I'm just glad you didn't bust her head through the wall. Sheetrock is kind of costly and not to mention all the hospital fees if you was to have given her a concussion."

The two men found Carlo's comment comical, because they bus tout in hysterical laughter.

"So . . . sorry sir. I didn't mean any disrespect," Rock managed to stamper out.

"No, no need for apologies," Carlos said with an arrogant smile. "Unless you plan on making my only daughter your concubine," he continued, replacing his broad smile with a hot frown that could've melted polar ice.

Rock didn't know what a concubine was, so he just nodded his head in agreement.

"Good, we have an understanding," he said while waving his hand at his two sons.

The two giants released him, then exited the room. Carlos followed behind them, then stopped short, retracing his steps.

He looked Rock squarely in the eyes and said, "You know back in Puerto Rico we have a saying or rather a longstanding tradition," he paused for more dramatic effect, as if that was needed, then continued, "you sleep with a man's daughter and consecrate a marriage, so with that said, welcome to the family."

Carlos left the room.

Rock didn't know it at the time, but Carlos was a man to be feared and respected. He not only owned the grocery store on the corner of Central Avenue and Ninth Street, but he owned the entire corner. A corner that produced almost seventy-thousand dollars a day profit in powdered and crack cocaine sales.

On the down low, Carlos and his sons supplied most of the drug dealers in the area with high quality Colombian cocaine.

Rock's heart was racing; however he wasn't scared. He knew they wouldn't have killed him right there, in the middle of his daughter's bedroom.

Suddenly, Maria walked into the room but stopped short when she noticed the screwed up look plastered on Rock's face.

"AHH ONNNNH, WHA THAPPENED. I KNOW MY BROTHERS AIN'T SAY NOTING TO YOU?" she yelled, then turned around talking even louder. Only this time in Spanish.

Rock sneaked up behind her and wrapped his arms around her waist. "No baby, everything's fine," he whispered in her ear, then flicked his tongue in it.

Maria trembled and almost dropped the drink that she had for him. She broke free from his seductive embrace, then handed him the glass filed with orange soda on the rocks. He gulped it down in one try, then returned the empty glass.

She took it, inspected it, then said, "Damn baby, you sure was thirsty."

"It's all your fault. You the one drained me of all my fluids." They both laughed, then Maria told him to put some clothes on before her mother came upstairs and saw him naked.

That would be a hell of a way to introduce himself, Rock thought to himself.

He got dressed, and Maria grabbed him by the hand and dragged him down the hallway closely behind herself. "Come on, I'm going to introduce you to my familia."

She got to her father's door, opened it slightly, then peeked in. She saw her father and two older brothers loading an arsenal of semi-automatic weapons, then quickly closed the door. "Oh, they busy right now," she said, dragging him with her down the steps. "Come on, I'm gone introduce you to me momma."

She peeked in on her mother, Maria senior. She was in the kitchen standing over a hot stove cooking. She was wearing a long floral printed blue dress and apron over her shorty pudgy frame.

Though she was shorter than her daughter, Rock noticed that her shortness didn't take away from her plump ass. The long loose fitting dress couldn't even hide it. Rock imagined that nothing Maria senior wore would be able to cover up that asset. I mean if Maria was Serena, then her mother was Buffie the body.

She called to her mother in Spanish, embraced her in a hug, then asked what she was cooking. She looked into the wide, round mouth of the pot on the stove. It was filled with boiling water and a large mayonnaise bottle occupied the center of it.

Maria could tell that the coke that she was cooking up was just about finished, by the Crisco colored oil that floated to the top.

Her mother quickly reduced the flame, added baking soda to the substance, then grabbed the lid of the jar with a hand towel and began to swish the mixture around in a circular motion. Seconds later she turned her water off, then added five large ice cubes to the mixture.

Maria was transfixed on the coke cooking process. So transfixed in fact that she had totally forgotten about her new lover.

Rock was standing in the entranceway of the kitchen, watching them and absorbing the entire scene. It wasn't until Maria's two pugnacious brothers sneaked up behind him with their guns drawn and had said in Spanish, "DON'T MOVE!" that she remembered he was still there.

One of the brothers pressed a shiny .45 automatic to the back of Rock's head.

His heart was racing, and he was beginning to perspire. He was scared, more frightened than a Blood member at a L.A. Crip meeting.

He thought about whirling around on his feet and attempting to disarm him, however quickly dismissed that idea, knowing that would only cause his brains to get spilled all over the kitchen floor.

I can't believe that I'm about to go out like a sucker, he thought to himself. And all over some pussy. I mean damn the pussy was good, but by no means good enough to lose my life for.

Rock put his hands up in hopes that that would be enough of a distraction to give him the split second he needed to execute his plan.

What plan? He really didn't know what he would do. The only thing that he knew for sure was if he was going to go out, it wouldn't be like a sucker. He would fight with every inch of his being.

Suddenly, Rock turned on his heels to face his killer.

With the barrel of the large .45 automatic still pointed at him, he heard Maria yell something behind him in Spanish.

This was it, he thought to himself. *The moment of truth, fight or flight, life or death.*

www.ingramcontent.com/pod-product-compliance
Lightning Source LLC
Chambersburg PA
CBHW071603110726
47908CB00007B/2228